CW00956613

RICH DUST

RICH DUST

GEORGE GREENFIELD

HOUSE OF STRATUS

This edition published in 2002 by House of Stratus, an imprint of House of Stratus Ltd, Thirsk Industrial Park, York Road, Thirsk, North Yorkshire, YO7 3BX, UK.
Also at: House of Stratus Inc., 2 Neptune Road, Poughkeepsie, NY 12601, USA.

www.houseofstratus.com

Typeset, printed and bound by House of Stratus.

A catalogue record for this book is available from the British Library and the Library of Congress.

ISBN 0-7551-0433-1

Contents

'On George Greenfield'
by Sir Ranulph Fiennes

George Greenfield was born in 1917. His forebears were farmers in the garden of Kent and George remained a loyal Kentish Man throughout his life.

After school at King's School Rochester, George went up to Downing College, Cambridge, to read his favourite subject, English Literature. There he came under the tutorage of the famous F R Leavis, who proved to be a huge influence, and encouraged him towards a career in academia.

George was certainly above-average clever and took a Double First degree in the language which he loved both to read and to write. His abilities did not go unnoticed and the senior tutor at Downing College had George lined up to be a spy when the war broke out. 'Join intelligence,' he said, 'and you'll be comfortable, safe and able to use your brains.'

Instead George joined the Infantry, training under various merciless sergeant-instructors, including the great cricketer, Len Hutton. He joined the oldest of all infantry regiments, the Buffs, his local Kent regiment, and became, in his own words, 'a temporary officer and gentleman.'

Over those early-war months, George's home was bombed by the Luftwaffe, he was machine-gunned by a Messerschmitt at Manston, and shelled by long-range artillery from across the Channel. In 1942 the Buffs were posted to the Eighth Army in Egypt, and George's platoon dug in along the edge of the Qattara Depression a few hundred yards from the forward Afrika Korps trenches. At night, the tune of Lily Marlene clearly audible in the dark air, George's task was to lead patrols through the barbed wire into no man's land to reconnoitre German positions.

The Buffs suffered bad casualties and George was promoted to regimental intelligence officer, and as such he had a very dramatic time with numerous narrow escapes. He fought through the key battle of El Alamein and on one occasion was blown up by mines twice in one day. Whilst others were killed and maimed all about him, he somehow managed to survive. He went on to become a senior staff officer, was present at the fateful Tehran summit of Stalin, Churchill and Roosevelt and travelled all over the Middle East before being posted as GSO2 to Cyprus in June 1945.

A month after being demobbed George was gazing at a window display in Hatchards when a wartime friend appeared. They lunched and George revealed his intentions of becoming a schoolteacher. His friend, however, had other ideas: 'My father owns Hatchards and has just bought a publishing house. He's looking for someone to run it. Why not you?'

And so George spent the next six years as supremo of T Werner Laurie Publishers at an annual salary of a thousand pounds. To begin with he was of course ignorant of anything to do with the book trade. Even the word 'blurb' meant nothing to him. But he learned fast and would surely have made it to the very top of the publishing world had he not been enticed away by his old friend and fellow Desert Rat, Innes Rose, to become a partner in the literary agents, John Farquharson.

Of this new departure, George himself said: 'Six years to the day after I joined Werner Laurie, I said goodbye to publishing and jumped over the fence into the new world of "ten per cent".' And so he was to become one of the sharks of the book pond. His years as a publisher had taught him many lessons that were to help him become the very best in the agency business. (Looking back on his successes he later wrote with some pride, 'I could best be classified as an aged cuckoo, having often slipped my authors into the nests of unsuspecting publishers!')

In no time at all in his new role as agent, George started to reach for the sky. He wrote to Enid Blyton out of the blue to ask if he could reprint any of her titles. They remained in close cahoots thereafter until her death. He collected a fine stable of American authors including Barbara Taylor Bradford and Sidney Sheldon; Morris, West, Jilly Cooper and Russell Braddon joined him, each with their very different style of writing. Of Russell Braddon's *The Naked Island*, written at George's instigation, he wrote, 'It was a grim and exhilarating account which proved the indestructibility of the human spirit. If I ever had to justify my years by citing just one book for which I was personally responsible, it would be *The Naked Island*.'

On one occasion I tried some agenting work of my own. News of this reached George's ears and he soon sent me a sharp note saying, 'If you keep a dog there's no point in doing your own barking.' This was the only Greenfield chastisement I received in twenty years.

George held sway in one or two specialist fields. These included autobiographies of English actors, including David Niven and Rex Harrison, and great sportsmen such as Peter May, Garfield Sobers, Gary Player, Ritchie Benaud and Stirling Moss.

In the field of expeditions, British and Commonwealth originated, George was often more than the literary agent; he was often the man behind the original idea. At lunch one day in the early seventies, he suggested to my wife that, 'a journey simply waiting to be attempted is the circumnavigation of the globe.' The spark came from George – a spark that was to cost us the next ten years of our lives. Such were his powers of inspiration!

George was also agent and mentor to Francis Chichester, Ed Hillary, Wally Herbert, Vivian Fuchs, Robin Knox-Johnston and Chris Bonington. Chris tells a story which occurred at the end of his successful 1975 expedition to ascend Everest's south-west face. George and Alan Tritton (the honorary treasurer of many such expeditions) accompanied the climbers back from their base camp to Namche Bazar. Once there, a rare plane came to take them to a Kathmandu Ambassadorial party in their honour. However the Pakistani Ambassador and his family then arrived and, claiming diplomatic privilege due to 'an urgent event', took over their plane. They were left stranded and missed the party. Some time later they discovered that the 'urgent event' was in fact their very own party in Kathmandu! George savoured the humour of that incident for many a year.

George held a special place in the hearts of many explorers including Vivian Fuchs, for years George's opponent in their highly competitive squash games, who showed his appreciation of their friendship by naming a feature in Antarctica, Mount Greenfield.

George eventually came to own John Farquharson outright and, although it was purchased by Curtis Brown in 1982, he continued to run the company until he retired in 1986 after thirty-four years as an agent.

Not the sort to retire to spend the rest of his days cultivating roses, George signed on at University College, London for a doctorate in the post-war novel. This led to his book, *Scribblers for Bread*, a deeply informed survey of how the world of agents and publishers had evolved since 1945. He went on to pen two wonderful memoirs: one about his early years, entitled *Chasing the Beast*, and then a highly entertaining collection of anecdotes called *A Smattering of Monsters* which gave a refreshingly new insight into the lives of many of his famous clients.

Of course his retirement was in name only for he continued to advise several of his erstwhile authors, remain a consultant for the Enid Blyton Estate and help many an American publisher with interests in Europe. He also tried to put Mrs Thatcher right when planning her memoirs – this was not a one hundred per cent success as she remained keen on her own ideas even when they conflicted with the voice of experience.

George obviously enjoyed his eighty-three years of life, his work, his family, and his friends, whether authors, adventurers, editors or fellow members of the Athenaeum. On 11 May 2000 he received a letter from 10 Downing Street informing him that his name had been submitted to Her Majesty the Queen with a recommendation that he be appointed a Member of the Order of the British Empire.

Unfortunately this honour cannot be given posthumously but there are many who will be pleased to know that his country realised his great worth in so many ways.

From the speech given by Sir Ranulph Fiennes on the occasion of George Greenfield's memorial service, 2000

'On George Greenfield'
by Ed Victor

In May of 1967, I arrived at Jonathan Cape Ltd with a new job and clean desk. In order to make myself useful, I decided to see whether I could get some advances refunded on overdue contracts. One of these recalcitrant authors was represented by George Greenfield, whose immediate response to my letter was to return his commission and urge his client to return the advance. I was so impressed by the swiftness and integrity of his reaction, that I asked him to a lunch, over which we agreed to go forward with the same book only by another of his writers. That began a relationship which culminated, seven years later, in George asking me to cross the then non-porous border between publishing and agenting by joining him at John Farquharson Ltd.

George was, without question, the best and brightest agent of his day in London. He was as tough as they came, but never left a scar. He always wanted the publisher to smile as broadly as he did at the end of a negotiation. He loved to strategise – preferably over a scotch and a cigar in the early evening – and his polite, even courtly demeanour belied the nimblest and toughest of minds. His authors loved him…and rightly so, for he was the perfect mentor because he gave unfettered, absolutely serious attention to their concerns. He also taught by example, as I learned so much just by watching and listening to him. George always knew just what he wanted for his authors, and he usually knew where he could get it. There was nobody better than him at 'finding the customer'. This involved a real fingertip feel for the work in question and then a virtually encyclopedic knowledge of which editor at which publishing house would be the right partner in the deal. Because he was so widely respected on both sides of the Great Divide – much greater then than it is now! – between agenting and publishing, he was uniquely suited to bringing two sides together in a mutually successful marriage.

I always thought that, if I ever wrote a book, I would have wanted George, above all others, to be my agent…so it was a great joy to me that, at the end of his life, he asked me to be the agent for his new novel. I know how happy it made him that the deal for its publication – the last of our many collaborations – was concluded just days before his death.

Ed Victor, 2000

Preface

A bet brought about my first novel. Second Battalion The Buffs had suffered quite heavy casualties during the Battle of Alamein and was pulled back to rest and refit. In January 1943, I was in a tent on the snowy slopes of a Persian mountain, arguing loudly with John Johnson. Books were rare and doubly precious. Both of us had just read a battered paperback copy of John Brophy's *Immortal Sergeant*. It was well written, but the technical desert warfare material was hopelessly out of date.

A one-time student of the great Dr F R Leavis, I was laying down the literary law. Those who could write, I argued, didn't know the real facts; those who knew probably couldn't write. John, the brother of Celia Johnson, the actress, had been a junior editor at Jonathan Cape before the war. He called my bluff by betting me five shillings – big money in those far-off days – that I couldn't write a successful war novel. That next afternoon, I sat in the back of a fifteen-hundredweight truck and, using an

Italian typewriter I had 'liberated', banged out the first
sentence: 'West of Alexandria lies the unfriendly desert.'
Most afternoons if I was off duty, I pushed on in my
innocence until, forty thousand words later, came 'The
End'.

John, who was to become a distinguished literary agent
after the war, read the script and quite liked it. But the big
test was – would it get published? He wrote to his friends
at Jonathan Cape to recommend *Desert Episode*, and I sent
them the typescript by surface mail. The Mediterranean
was still closed to Allied shipping, which had to go
round the Cape and up the length of the Atlantic, a prey to
Japanese submarine on the southern journey and to U-boats
on the second leg.

Several months later, the script came back, accompanied
by a crisp letter from the publishers, saying it read like a
collection of short stories. Dejected, I chucked the battered
pages, my only copy, into the bottom of an old kitbag.

Half a year went by. I was stuck in a transit camp
near the Iraqi border for three days. There were no books
to be had and I was a voracious reader. Finding an old
Army magazine, I read every word down to the small
advertisements at the back. The House of Macmillan was
about to celebrate its centenary by giving an award for
fiction and one for non-fiction, confined to members of the
Forces. On an impulse, I dug out the script of *Desert
Episode* and sent it off once more.

Silence. Months and months of silence. I learned much later that it had been acknowledged but I had moved nearly a thousand miles since sending the parcel and the publishers' letter never caught up with me. I wrote it off in my mind, thinking a German U-boat must have sunk the merchant ship containing my precious one and only copy.

In March 1945 I was at the staff college in Haifa. After breakfast one morning, a fellow student, reading *The Palestine Post*, the English language local paper, asked, 'Have you got a brother in your regiment?'

I said, 'No, I haven't got a brother.'

'Well then, who the hell's this Greenfield who's won the Macmillan Centenary Award?'

There was an amusing sequel. At the staff college in those days, perhaps still, you had to write a longish essay early on in the course and another towards the end. My first effort had been awarded a 'D'. Oddly enough, word of the Macmillan Award having circulated, my second essay ended up with an 'A'.

Desert Episode was well-reviewed and sold over thirty-five thousand copies in the hardback edition. In paperback it later sold more than four hundred and fifty thousand copies during the nineteen-fifties' boom. Perhaps more importantly, its existence helped me to a post-war career in the book world.

Over fifty years and half a dozen books later, I happened to read the Dorothy L Sayers version of 'The Song of

Roland', followed by the biography of General Freyberg, VC, the great New Zealand desert general. An idea for a shortish novel struck me. I wanted to write something that, to transpose John Donne, 'would make me end where I begun.'

Rich Dust is the result.

George Greenfield, 2000

Rich Dust

'If I should die, think only this of me:
That there's some corner of a foreign field
That is for ever England. There shall be
In that rich earth a richer dust concealed.'

From 'The Soldier' by Rupert Brooke

Prologue

I stood outside the gates of the Duke of York's Barracks on the King's Road and waved at the taxi speeding along on the opposite side of the road. He didn't stop. Bastard. And then the deeper, more painful realisation hit home. This would be the last reunion for the survivors of Operation Scorpion. There were only four of us left.

The 27th of June 1999: the fifty-seventh anniversary of Scorpion and the fifty-second anniversary of the reunion club. At least, we had managed to hit the fifty mark. When I arrived, I had looked round the small table in the mess room at the Duke of York's. It was crazy to hire a room that would have seated at least forty – the numbers we would have expected five, ten years back – with three serving staff and a bar with an attendant, just for the four of us.

An easy routine had long been established. No regard to rank or seniority, you just mucked in together. It was like the old days in the sergeants' mess at Christmas, when everyone from the commanding officer downwards took off his jacket or battledress blouse and chucked it on the heap. Eyes shut, you picked one out at random and wore it for the rest of the evening, so the CO might end up wearing a sergeant's blouse and a company sergeant-major might lark around with the CO's crown and pips.

The only formality at the reunion was the special toast. At the end of the meal, we would stand up for the loyal toast and then sit down again. The senior rank present, still sitting, would then say, 'Gentlemen, I give you the special toast. To Operation Scorpion and good men gone.' The others, also sitting, would raise their glasses and say, 'To Scorpion and good men gone.' Then we would drink and sit for a moment in silence, remembering the comrades who had died all too young, and feeling a twinge of guilt for having survived them.

But the reunions were not all doom and gloom. There was a lot of fun to be had, especially in the sixties and early seventies when Sir Paul Groombridge took part. He was a real card was Groombridge. Captured along with the other Scorpion survivors, he had spent three years in a German prisoner-of-war camp. Let out and given early demob, he had put all his Army money, a tidy sum, on a tip-off for Newmarket. Or so he later claimed. The outsider he had backed won and he was left with three thousand pounds, a small fortune in those days.

Groombridge had guessed London would have to be rebuilt once peace was fully established. So, he went round buying bombed-out corner properties and reselling them a few months later for nearly double what he had spent. Small deals led to bigger deals and eventually, backed by a friendly bank manager, who took a modest private cut, into very big property deals.

He was never quite in the Charles Clore class but for someone who had emigrated from Mile End Road, he was rich enough. The chauffeur-driven gleaming Rolls Royce would park inside the big gates of the Duke of York's Barracks and deposit Sir Paul (knighted through one of Harold Wilson's so-called 'dodgy lists') at the reunion where he would have sent a magnum or two of vintage champagne in advance. The lads teased him, of course, but there seemed to be a touch of respect mixed up in the banter.

Then came the mid-seventies crash. Even people as acute as Jim Slater were caught napping. Groombridge was completely overstretched. He had tried to bluff things out with the bank, which suddenly was not quite so friendly as before. In the end, he had to go bankrupt. He did turn up at the next reunion, riding a bicycle, and took the jesting in good heart. But that was the last we saw of him. He had made his sergeant-major, on the latter's retirement from the Regular Army, head of security for his many properties. When Groombridge was riding high, CSM Hogben never turned up to the annual reunion; but once the bubble had burst, 'Old Piggy', as his friends called him, was back, all grins and the thumping of biceps.

This year, June 1999, I was the senior one present of the four of us. I had been a captain, second-in-command of B Company 1st Kents, back in the desert all that while ago. The others were Shakesy Roberts, Daffy Norman and Lakri Wood. Shakesy had been a pre-war regular, who had contracted malaria while serving in India. Apparently, he then had a fit of the shakes, hence the nickname. Now his hands shook all the time with a fine tremor. It had taken him ages to spear the slice of chicken breast with his fork and arduously cut off a piece. He must be about eighty.

Daffy's initials were DPHN and when he joined the Battalion in 1940, aged twenty, the drill sergeant christened him 'Daphne'. This had stuck and time had slurred it to 'Daffy'. I remembered an assault course on the steep side of Bluebell Hill, a few miles from the depot. Everyone had to tackle it in full fighting gear, pack on the back, rifle and bayonet. Eighteen minutes was the pass time. (General Montgomery's motto was 'fighting fit and fit to fight' – whatever that might mean.) But if you took a second longer, you were out. I had scrambled through at something over seventeen minutes; Daffy Norman had held the battalion record at eleven and a half minutes. He simply bounced with vitality then. Now he spent almost the entire lunch telling us about the hip replacement he needed. He had been on the waiting list since the autumn of 1998, over nine months ago, and his GP had told him last week that he might have to wait as long again. The pain was continual, as his screwed-up face revealed. He walked, what walking he could manage, with a pronounced limp.

Like Shakesy, Lakri Wood was a pre-war regular. In India, he had been nicknamed 'Lakri' after the Urdu word for 'wood'. He had been a senior corporal in June 1942 and ended up as RSM on one of the wartime battalions. He was the oldest of the four of us – eighty-three, I reckoned – and looked much the fittest. I was eighty-two. Last year, I had found the hundred-yard trudge from the portico of the Duke of York's mess building to the main gates about as much as I could cope with. This year, I had to pause three or four times, and pretend to be watching the prep school children in their reddish-brown uniforms playing ball games on the pitch alongside as I fought to get my breath back. It was a survival of the unfittest, I thought.

Shakespeare was wrong. It is not a case that 'old men forget'. They well remember – at least, the distant past. They may forget where they left their spectacles five minutes ago but any vital event fifty years back is still vivid in their minds. No, the real problem is that old men die off and they take their secrets to the grave. In the mid-nineties, when there was still a lot of fun at our reunions and a positive spirit, I had hoped that we might keep going until the millennium.

Now it is beginning to look as though only Lakri will be around for next year's celebration, let alone the one twelve months later. When I finally managed to flag down a taxi outside the Duke of York's Barracks and slumped breathless onto the back seat, I made a vow. Before it was too late, I would set down the full story of Operation Scorpion. I knew all the anecdotes, the stories and the facts, official and unofficial, and, living not too far from the regimental depot, I would have easy access to 1st Battalion's war diaries and official reports. I might have to take a few extra pills a day to keep me mobile – but so what?

No waffle, no bullshit. Short and sharp, that is the aim. I shall take the liberty of playing God by describing the thoughts and feelings of the main characters, as well as my own. This may seem presumptuous, but men in action, particularly those few on a special mission, learn to sense what their comrades are thinking and feeling, often by looking into their own hearts.

So this is what happened all those years ago in a forgotten corner of a vast desert.

Dan Glenister, 1999

1

The Brigadier's staff car was backed into a small hollow. Groundsheets, slung on either side over a central pole, provided shelter and were a cover for the electric light that was attached to the back of the front seats. Camouflage netting, draped over the groundsheets and stretched out on either side of the car, finished off the disguise.

The Brigadier sat in one of the back seats, our Commanding Officer alongside him. The Brigade Major half-sat, half-knelt on the passenger seat in front. Notebook in left hand, he had twisted round to face his two senior officers.

The Brigadier was quietly saying, 'It's the same old story, Mike. Order, counter-order, disorder. I'm just back from Corps with all the news. It seems the Auk has fired General Ritchie and taken personal control of the Eighth Army.'

'What?' exploded the CO.

'No fooling.'

'But General Auchinleck's basically a desk-man, isn't he? He hasn't been fired at in anger since – since when?'

The Brigadier sighed, 'Since a long time. But at least he's got a plan. Let's face it, we'll never stop Rommel out in the open. He's got better guns, better tanks and, God knows, better tactics, so far. The Auk's plan is to withdraw the Eighth Army to El Alamein and make a stand there.'

'Alamein? Isn't that one of those settlements near the Egyptian border?'

'Right.' Looking up at the Brigade Major, the Brigadier said, 'Tell the Colonel, Peter. Come on now – your best Staff College polish.'

The young man said, 'There's a natural escarpment, sir, running more or less north and south from Alamein in the north to El Himeimat in the south. And immediately south of Himeimat is the Qattara Depression, impassable to vehicles. So, if we can hold Alamein, we can hold all of Egypt and most of the Middle East.'

The CO nodded. He wondered why he had been summoned at this ungodly hour, when there was so much to look after with his own troops, to receive a geography lesson. Or was it a history lesson?

The Brigadier went on, 'The New Zealand Division was surrounded by 21 Panzer and others. They smashed their way out – bloody marvellous fighters! – and are holding the southern flank as they pull back towards Alamein. Several

'Do I know any of them?'

'Major Lapledge is the company commander, Captain Glenister his second in command.'

'Yes, of course, I know them both. Wasn't Glenister your battalion Intelligence Officer a short while back? I thought so. He used to come to Brigade for briefings. Seemed a good sort. My quartermaster's been rounding up spare water and rations to be delivered to your HQ within the hour. By the way, go easy on the chahguls – they're so wasteful.'

A chahgul was roughly the size and shape of a hot-water bottle. It was made of semi-porous webbing and tied to the outside of trucks. The water slowly seeped through its webbing cover which was kept deliciously cool by the truck's forward motion. But evaporation caused a waste.

'One last word, Mike,' the Brigadier said. 'The Matruh wadi's about a mile and a half from your present location. Most of the troops will have to leg it. I want the transport kept down to a bare minimum. A medical truck, a signals truck and a fifteen hundredweight to carry the mortars, spare blankets, rations – that sort of thing. That's your lot. We don't want to alert the Afrika Korps by sounding like Piccadilly Circus on Boat Race night.'

There was a pause. The CO said, 'Could I have a word?'

The Brigadier glanced at him and then across at the Brigade Major, who was still scribbling down his notes. 'OK, Peter, that's it. We'll go through the details later.'

The Brigade Major looked up, surprised, saw the two old friends wanted shot of him, said, 'Sir' sharply and bundled out of the staff car.

When he was well out of earshot, the Brigadier said, 'That young man will go far.'

'But not far enough for your liking?'

'Right first time. He's so into doing it by the book, so damned ambitious. Deep down, he couldn't care less for his regiment – or yours or mine. He wants promotion and nothing'll faze him. But enough of him. I was just thinking…'

The CO was getting a shade impatient. There was a lot to do and time was running on. 'Yes?' he said urgently.

'Sorry, Mike, I'll cut it short. Point is this. If I can ease young Peter out – and I will – could I have your permission to put in for Major Lapledge as brigade major? I know he's a first-rate company commander but I reckon he could do with a spell as a brigade major when we get settled at El Alamein. It all adds to his CV.'

'So you want to grab one of my best – perhaps, the best – officers. But I couldn't stand in his way. Yes, of course you have my permission. Mind you, we're both supposing he survives Scorpion.'

'Of course. Mike, you're a gentleman. Lapledge looks the surviving kind to me. There may even be a medal in it for him when Scorpion is over.'

18

other divisions are to start moving back at first light tomorrow. The way the Eighth Army is scattered, it's anything from eighty to ninety miles to their final destination. They need *time* – and as much as possible. Which is where you come in, Mike.

'About two miles west of here, between us and Rommel, there's a longish narrow wadi. You probably don't have a clear impression of it – I certainly don't – because we all came through split-arse with Jerry not far behind. But I've got a section of the Long Range Desert Group attached and they've just done a detailed reconnaissance. It seems ideal for the purpose. Peter here's going to give you a breakdown of the area. All yours, Peter.'

The Brigade Major glanced at his notes and then continued. 'The coastal track runs through the wadi, sir. It is about a hundred yards long, perhaps a shade more. It is about a furlong from the actual coast but the whole of the north side beyond the wadi consists of salt pans. The LRDG reckon that area is no good for tracked vehicles. But they have warned us that when the sun is up and bright, the dazzle from the surface salt could be quite dangerous. They advise goggles for any men stationed on the north side of the wadi.

'There is a patch of very soft sand immediately south of the wadi and then the Minqar Qaim escarpment, which runs roughly west north-west to east south-east. It does serve one good purpose. Any part of the Afrika Korps trying to encircle the wadi would be deflected way down south. I think that's the gist of it, sir.'

'You get the point, Mike?' the Brigadier asked the CO. 'There's no way for enemy armour north of the wadi. If they do attempt to push on south of it, first there's the soft sand and then a steep escarpment. Too steep for armour. You follow? Rommel's only got one way to go. Through the wadi. OK, we could mine the track inside the wadi but how long would that stop Jerry? Two hours, three at the most? Corps says we've got to deny it to the enemy for the whole day. Tomorrow.'

'I'm beginning to get the message,' said the CO.

'Too damn right. Mike, we know the Afrika Korps tends to stay put at night, especially in strange territory. So if we can hold the wadi throughout the daylight hours tomorrow, we'll gain another nine hours of darkness. Added to the rest of tonight, that's a total of almost forty hours. Vital hours in which Eighth Army Corps and the others fall back towards El Alamein.

'So these are my orders. Make notes, will you, Peter. Colonel Nichols, as officer commanding 1st Kents you will nominate your best company. Their intention: to occupy and hold the Matruh wadi until nightfall – 20.30 hours – tomorrow, 27 June. They will be reinforced with a troop of the Royal Horse Artillery, a section of sappers, a detachment from Signals and a field-dressing station. Oh yes, and a standby team from the Long Range Desert

Group to act as link between the forward company and your HQ.'

'What about our radio sets, sir?'

'Sorry, Mike, I should have mentioned this. Total radio silence throughout the operation.'

'Can I raise a point?' the CO asked.

'Fire away.'

'Let's suppose they do advance and my people have to open fire. From that moment, all surprise is lost. What on earth's the point in keeping radio silence after that?'

The Brigadier rubbed his moustache with a knuckle as he pondered. 'Good point, Mike. Right, cancel that last order. Radio silence may be broken – but only to report a major event. I'll sort things out with division and corps, so unless you hear from me within the hour, forget the original order.'

'You will need a code name, sir,' said the Brigade Major.

'I was coming to that.' Pause. 'How about Scorpion, Mike?'

'Great, sir. Let's hope we can sting 'em where it hurts!'

The Brigade Major said to the Brigadier, 'Excuse me, sir, but code names are supposed to be picked at random and not describe the actual event.'

'Peter, you're not in staff college now,' said the Brigadier with more than a hint of exasperation in his voice. 'You've rejoined the real world. When they start using the code name, they'll have the enemy in their sights. The whole

15

bloody Afrika Korps will already know they've got a fight on their hands! Now, one way you could be useful to the CO here. Any intelligence on who the immediate opposition is?'

'The LRDG reckon there are elements of 15 Panzer Division and 90 Light closest to the wadi.'

The Brigadier said, 'They're good. Damn good. But not better. I wouldn't have picked out the Kents if I hadn't thought they'd see off the opposition! OK, Mike, any questions?'

The CO scratched his chin and thought for a moment. The damned sand got everywhere. He could feel it in the crevices of his ears, matting together the short hairs on the back of his neck, in his eyebrows, everywhere. Bloody desert, bloody war and a bloody job for B Company. He had already decided in his mind it would be B to plug the gap. 'No, sir,' he finally said. 'It's pretty straightforward. I take it the spare parts – the RHA troop, the sappers and the signals team – will find their own way up to the sharp end.'

'Apologies,' said the Brigadier, 'I should have mentioned this earlier. They are moving up to your battalion HQ right now. When you have chosen your company commander for Operation Scorpion, they will come immediately under his command. Incidentally, it's entirely up to you and I wouldn't dream of interfering but, as a matter of interest, have you thought which company you'll nominate?'

'B Company, sir.'

'Do I know any of them?'

'Major Lapledge is the company commander, Captain Glenister his second in command.'

'Yes, of course, I know them both. Wasn't Glenister your battalion Intelligence Officer a short while back? I thought so. He used to come to Brigade for briefings. Seemed a good sort. My quartermaster's been rounding up spare water and rations to be delivered to your HQ within the hour. By the way, go easy on the chahguls – they're so wasteful.'

A chahgul was roughly the size and shape of a hot-water bottle. It was made of semi-porous webbing and tied to the outside of trucks. The water slowly seeped through its webbing cover which was kept deliciously cool by the truck's forward motion. But evaporation caused a waste.

'One last word, Mike,' the Brigadier said. 'The Matruh wadi's about a mile and a half from your present location. Most of the troops will have to leg it. I want the transport kept down to a bare minimum. A medical truck, a signals truck and a fifteen hundredweight to carry the mortars, spare blankets, rations – that sort of thing. That's your lot. We don't want to alert the Afrika Korps by sounding like Piccadilly Circus on Boat Race night.'

There was a pause. The CO said, 'Could I have a word?'

The Brigadier glanced at him and then across at the Brigade Major, who was still scribbling down his notes. 'OK, Peter, that's it. We'll go through the details later.'

17

The Brigade Major looked up, surprised, saw the two old friends wanted shot of him, said, 'Sir' sharply and bundled out of the staff car.

When he was well out of earshot, the Brigadier said, 'That young man will go far.'

'But not far enough for your liking?'

'Right first time. He's so into doing it by the book, so damned ambitious. Deep down, he couldn't care less for his regiment – or yours or mine. He wants promotion and nothing'll faze him. But enough of him. I was just thinking...'

The CO was getting a shade impatient. There was a lot to do and time was running on. 'Yes?' he said urgently.

'Sorry, Mike, I'll cut it short. Point is this. If I can ease young Peter out – and I will – could I have your permission to put in for Major Lapledge as brigade major? I know he's a first-rate company commander but I reckon he could do with a spell as a brigade major when we get settled at El Alamein. It all adds to his CV.'

'So you want to grab one of my best – perhaps, the best – officers. But I couldn't stand in his way. Yes, of course you have my permission. Mind you, we're both supposing he survives Scorpion.'

'Of course. Mike, you're a gentleman. Lapledge looks the surviving kind to me. There may even be a medal in it for him when Scorpion is over.'

18

Seeing they had finished the official business, the CO said, 'I'd better be on my way. What we've just discussed is between the two of us – right?'

'Indeed.'

The CO relaxed. 'You always were a wily devil, Hoppy. I never could read you. My impression is you seem chipper over the op. But knowing you, that could be a load of bullshit, of course. To tell you the truth, I'm feeling a bit down about it, myself. Yes. We can put the cork in the bottle, all right, but no one can guarantee Rommel won't just smash the bottle. You were a bit of a gambler in your Sandhurst days – what odds would you give my B Company? Losing half of them? Evens? Less than evens? Losing the lot? You tell me.'

The Brigadier smiled. He understood the CO's apprehensions. 'I know, Mike. Don't forget I commanded a battalion myself for close on two years. They're your men, your comrades. Losing any of 'em is like losing a member of the family. That's the bloody thing about war. In a tough situation, you have to put your best men forward. And they get the casualties. But I don't have to tell you. You've known the score all along. Yours is the best battalion in the brigade – and that's thanks to you, Mike – and you tell me B Company's your best company. Right now we need the best. Somehow, God knows how, they've got to hang on in that bloody wadi until nightfall tomorrow. If they do, they just might have saved the whole Eighth

19

Army. And even if they don't, B Company will have held the enemy back for at least a few hours. It all helps.'

'Thanks, Hoppy,' the CO smiled back. 'The lousiest part of this job is nominating good men for nasty jobs.'

As he opened the staff car's door, the Brigadier said, 'Goodnight, Mike – and good luck.'

'I'll pass that last bit on to B Company.'

The Brigadier looked at him levelly. 'D'you think I enjoy giving "last man, last round" orders?'

2

The moon was high over the Mediterranean amid a glitter of stars. Major Roland Lapledge had just finished his operational orders and turned to his second-in-command, Captain Dan Glenister. 'Dan, will you look after the main body? They should be in a state of readiness – but need to stay put for thirty minutes. It'll take me that long to complete a forward recce. If you hear shooting up ahead, fan out and stand by. If all's quiet by then, move 'em up. On foot, of course, apart from the back-up trucks. The track itself looks pretty firm but if you feel the approach march is getting too noisy, they could always go single file in the sand on either side of the track. Anyway, it's all yours. See you later.'

Lapledge climbed into the jeep, which sounded ominously loud as it slid away into the night, throwing a plume of sand dust behind it. Dan noticed, sitting in the back of the jeep, the RHA lieutenant, Jocelyn Abbeyfield, and the sapper sergeant.

Abbeyfield, with his fair hair and pink cheeks, looked about sixteen but he wore the purple and white ribbon of the Military Cross with a rosette in its centre to denote a bar to the medal. It was a good time to respect courage. He was also wearing suede desert boots, 'brothel creepers' as they had become known.

Major Lapledge had sent a small fighting patrol ahead to scour the wadi for unpleasant surprises. As the jeep approached, the corporal in charge of the patrol stood up and waved his arms over his head. The coast was clear. The jeep pulled up and the Major told his driver to turn into the shadows, switch off and wait. The moon was now near its apex, shedding a light so bright you could read by it. The moonlight cast black blotches of shadow, and in the distance a kind of suffused glow. The temperature had dropped to a few degrees above freezing.

The small party walked slowly along the track as it entered the Matruh wadi. At the entrance, the track was about twenty feet wide; firm earth and small stones pressed down by centuries of walking feet, camels, mules and, latterly, tanks and trucks. On either side, sandy hillocks, their tops perhaps seven or eight feet above the track levels, stretched in a wavering line. The route ran straight for about forty paces and then widened out into an irregular circle, its diameter around thirty-five yards. On the far side, the enemy side, it converged abruptly into a track somewhat narrower. Almost as compensation, both sides were taller and steeper. Twenty paces on from the wider area, the track that had been running almost straight jinked suddenly to the left, southward.

'Leave to speak, sir?' asked Lieutenant Abbeyfield.

The Major looked at him abruptly. Was the kid pulling his leg? 'Right,' he said. 'Speak.'

'This could be a good site for my AFVs.'

'You reckon?'

'Yes. There's a good line of fire ahead and useful cover on the left, the south side.'

Major Lapledge walked up to him until their shoulders were almost touching. He squinted along the arm the young man held out, parallel with the ground. 'I see what you mean. Fine, that's got the heavy stuff sorted out. Leave a marker here, will you? I'd like you to continue the recce, so you'll know where the rest of us fit in. Right, let's press on.'

The small group moved on in the cold, hard moonlight, pausing every now and then as the Major clambered up the sliding slopes of sand on either side of the wadi, to peer over the crests and occasionally take a compass bearing. The moon was at its height, casting a strange sheen across the dun-coloured desert. It drew pools of shadow from small mounds and hollows. Exposed, the salt pans glittered, sparkle reflecting off the crystals.

Finally, he summoned the Royal Engineers sergeant. 'At ease, sarn't. I think you know the overall plan. We've got to deny this wadi to the enemy throughout the daylight hours tomorrow. From first light until perhaps twenty-hundred. Quite a task. At some point Rommel will try to push his armour through the wadi. It's his only short cut. You've brought some mines with you?'

'Sir. Only one problem – they're EP mines.'

The Major nodded. After almost exactly two years in the Western Desert, he knew about EP mines. But the sapper sergeant, like most military specialists, was not prepared to forego his moment of expertise. He said, 'EP is Egyptian Pattern. Mines assembled by wogs in Cairo. Some are so insensitive an elephant could waltz on 'em. Others so touchy, you only have to blow hard in their direction – and whoops! Nasty things.'

'Well, in that case I've got an unpleasant task for you and your squad. I want you and your squad to mine the track just where it enters the wadi on this side. As quietly as you can and make sure there are no tell-tale marks on the track itself after the job's done.'

The sergeant drew in his breath sharply as though about to swear, and then slowly exhaled. 'What about sympathetic detonation, sir? An enemy shell landing close to the mines could set them off. That's what I mean by sympathetic detonation, sir.'

24

'I didn't arrive on the last boat, sergeant. Understand one thing. The orders I give are orders and not a basis for discussion. Get cracking. Now.'

The sapper sergeant left at the double, lurching sideways in the soft sand alongside the track. Lieutenant Abbeyfield strolled over and said, 'With respect and all that stuff, sir, wouldn't it be better to stop 'em way out in the open, not on our own doorstep?'

The Major replied, 'Your way, we stop one tank. But they still come forward. My way, we also stop one tank. But it blocks the whole entrance to the wadi. Get it? To clear the track, Jerry will have to bring forward a tank removal unit. And all the time they're like ducks in a shooting gallery.'

'Why didn't I think of that first?'

'Modesty forbids me answering that one.'

They walked on in companionable silence. Lapledge, who didn't make friends easily, found himself taking to this young man. In this army, he thought, youth was hard to define. He himself was twenty-seven, five or six years older than Abbeyfield, who looked about eighteen. He had probably still been at school when war broke out. But a long war speeded the growing-up process. He, Lapledge, commissioned into the Regular Army in 1936, would still be a junior lieutenant now, had peace prevailed.

Back where the wadi widened out, they found the Company O Group waiting. There were the three junior officers commanding a platoon each, a sergeant from the Royal Signals, another from the Medical Corps and the Company Sergeant Major, Aaron Hogben, or 'Piggy', as he was known throughout the battalion. A pre-war regular, he had been a lance corporal with 2nd Kents before and during Dunkirk. Where some soldiers with indifferent leaders had thrown away their heavy rifles and ammunition pouches in their mad dash to escape the blitzkrieg, Hogben's men were fully equipped when they boarded the ship to safety. And that in spite of having had to fight their way out of a German cordon. He was a man of great common sense and an easy temperament, liked and respected by officers and other ranks.

As they approached the gathering, Roland prepared himself to address them. 'It's going to be a long night, so we might as well make ourselves comfortable while we can. At ease, gentlemen. I am Major Lapledge, officer commanding B Company, 1st Kents. Our intention is to deny the Afrika Korps passage through this wadi until nightfall tomorrow, 27 June. Approximately twenty-one-hundred hours. I have already arranged for the sappers to lay a small minefield across the track immediately west of the wadi. The plan – for those of you who haven't grasped it yet,' he shot a quick smile at Abbeyfield, 'is for the leading tank to blow itself up and block the entrance.

26

'The Royal Horse Artillery with its twenty-five-pounders is our main weapon against the tanks. Mr Abbeyfield here leads the RHA contingent and has already sited his weapons. He will need some supporting fire – a rifle section and a couple of brens. To be supplied by Mr Penfold's platoon. All right with you, Johnnie?'

'Right, sir.'

'When I've finished orders, have a word with Mr Abbeyfield and sort out just where he'd like your men placed.'

'Yes, sir.'

Roland Lapledge went on, 'There is a strong chance, almost a certainty, that when the enemy tanks get held up, their infantry will swan out on either side of the wadi and attack from the flanks. Units from 90 Light are supposed to be well forward. Most of us have met 'em before. They're good. So, to the three platoon commanders your instructions are to make sure you've got plenty of men with arcs of fire high up on the wadi banks on either side. Specially, the units towards the rear. On no account must they be allowed to encircle us on foot.

'You've all seen how the wadi is narrow at the front and rear but bulges out quite widely in the middle. In that area Company HQ will be located, along with the field-dressing station and Signals. Which reminds me. Absolute radio silence until fighting starts. No one will be more than about fifty yards from HQ, so have a runner standing by all the time.

'Get the troops digging in as soon as they know their locations. It'll break up their rest period, but they'll be thanking me tomorrow! Those Afrika Korps mortars can be too precise for comfort. I don't have to tell you to post sentries for the remainder of the night. As always, there will be a dawn stand-to. But no – repeat, no – warming up of the brens. The enemy must think the wadi's unoccupied for as long as possible. By which I mean – no brewing up before first light, no smoking, no naked lights at all. Ram that home to your men. Now, any questions?'

Penfold asked, 'Sir, what happens at nightfall tomorrow night?'

'Good point. Rommel's men don't like operating at night. We all know that from experience. So my hunch is they'll put in one last big effort in late afternoon, early evening. We see that off and then stay in position until darkness – or earlier recall by Division on the R/T. The LRDG will be liaising with us. There will be an orderly withdrawal with the wounded going first. All usable vehicles must be filled to capacity, so each of you try to give your trucks what shelter there is. One fighting unit – Number 6 Platoon – will be last out, along with Company HQ. Once the trucks are full, I'm afraid it's Shanks' pony for the rest of us. The LRDG has a couple of jeeps and will be ferrying the walkers in batches back to the main body.'

'Sir, you said Division might get on the blower and recall us earlier. Is there much chance of that?' asked Lieutenant Penfold.

'God knows, Johnnie. I suppose if there was a risk we'd be totally cut off. But basically, we've got to stick it out right here until twenty-hundred tomorrow night. It's what they used to call a last man, last round, situation.'

Penfold was going to say something funny. And then stopped himself. It wasn't a very funny situation.

'Right, gentlemen, we've all got a job to do. Let's get cracking. Good luck to all of us. The op has been code-named Scorpion, by the way.'

'Scorpion, sir?'

'Yes, Scorpion. We're to be the sting in the tail. Get it? Right, that's it. End of orders. Now get cracking and sort yourselves out.'

When they were alone, Roland said to Dan, 'Here's how I see it. I'll have a forward headquarters, basically just myself and that idiot Billows if he hasn't gone and got lost. I'll operate from where the wadi widens out up to the far end. Once things start, I reckon to be on the move most of the time. You'll look after the rear echelons, the dressing station, the sappers and so on. Your area of responsibility includes from where the widening starts back to the eastern end of the wadi. When action is joined, radio silence comes off, so we can keep in touch by runner or R/T. All right?

'Last thing, Dan. Once your people are in position, for Christ's sake, get some rest. Tomorrow is going to be a big day.'

3

Major Lapledge was taking one last look round at the forward defences, accompanied by CSM Hogben. The men had worked hard at digging their slit trenches, and had now completed almost all of them. The bren-gun sites might need adjusting under the harsher glare of daylight, but for the moment they seemed fair enough. On the whole, Lapledge felt satisfied.

His private self-congratulations proved short-lived as the Sergeant-Major interrupted his reverie and broke the silence of the night air around them. 'Just a thought, sir. Would it be worth sending out a two-man recce patrol? I don't mean to get right up to the enemy, sir. Just to go two or three hundred yards, roughly halfway into no man's land, and take some bearings on enemy activity?'

The Major was brought down to earth with a bump. It wasn't a bad idea. In fact, he should have thought of it himself.

'You're right, Sarn't-Major. Good idea. Why don't you organise it? Just two men from Mr Penfold's section, I think. If you have a problem, tell him I ordered it. They're not to stay out too long – two hours maximum. I want everyone to be rested up for tomorrow. All right?'

'Yes, sir.'

'Oh, and Sarn't-Major, if I'm wanted, I'll be back there with Mr Abbeyfield's RHA troop.'

'Sir!'

CSM Hogben liked and admired his company commander. The Major was generally a considerate man, and never ordered his men to undertake anything that he himself would not attempt. He was one of the old-fashioned breed of officers, a regular through and through, whose creed was his regiment. His only problem, 'Piggy' Hogben thought, was the high standard he imposed on himself. His rigid code demanded that he be the fittest, toughest, sharpest, bravest man in B Company. So far he had proved himself each time – but this operation still had a long way to go.

With these thoughts in mind, the CSM reported to Lieutenant Penfold and received his permission to 'borrow' Corporal 'Shakesy' Roberts and a private soldier named Peter Craig for a few hours that night. Craig was to act as the number two. He handed over the night compass he had 'liberated' from around the neck of an officer from another regiment, who had been killed in a night attack.

'Don't for Gawd's sake lose it, Roberts,' he said. 'Here, undo the lanyard thing and put it round your neck. Right, no weapons. Travel light and quiet. All you need, Craig, is a pencil and a couple of sheets of paper. OK? Now, Shakesy, I reckon you should go out on a bearing of two hundred and twenty degrees south-westish from here. There looks to be some nice dead ground two hundred, maybe two-fifty yards ahead. If I'm right, that could be a useful area to settle in. You got a good wrist-watch? Fine. Stay put an hour and a half, two hours maximum. Come back on the reverse bearing, which would be...' He paused and looked at the two men standing in front of him. 'Well, Craig? You got an idea in that thick skull?'

'Er – forty degrees, sir.'

Just a few years earlier, Private Craig had won an open scholarship in mathematics at Trinity College, Cambridge. He had gone on to gain a starred first in part one of the tripos, and would no doubt have been appointed a junior wrangler had he completed the course. But he had instead decided to enlist in the army and had chosen the infantry as the lowest form of intellectual life. At the appointments board sitting in the Senate House, he had been urged to rethink and use his manifest powers of deduction at the secret decoding centre set up in an old mansion in the Home Counties, but he had persisted in volunteering for the infantry. He had been flogging his brains through examinations year after year. Now they could have a good long rest.

'You know, Craig, you're not such a big fool as you look,' said the CSM. No one in the platoon or the company knew Craig's background.

'Thank you, sir, I think,' he said.

The CSM went on, 'You're not likely to bump into Jerry taking an after-dinner stroll but if you do, remember it's name, rank and number only. I know – you've heard that a hundred times but it's my duty to spell it out once again. And try to give the impression you're a couple of strays. You left the truck to go and have a crap and when you got back, the truck had moved on. Get it? We don't want them to know about Operation Scorpion.

'And that, in case you've managed to forget already, is the password. Scorpion. I'll warn the sentries to expect you around midnight. That's it. Any questions? No. Good luck – and bring those ugly mugs back safely.'

Corporal Roberts held the compass up to his right eye. As he rotated it slowly to his left, the numbers flashed past on the luminous dial – from two hundred and seventy degrees, due west, downwards to around two hundred and twenty. At two hundred and fifteen, he spotted a notch on the skyline, a rock formation, perhaps, or a fold in the sandy slope. He dropped to his knees and checked the bearing again. It was even clearer against the pale night sky, and would do well enough for the outward leg. If he kept slightly to the right, he would be on the bearing the Sergeant-Major had nominated.

No man's land looked starkly bare under the baleful light of the moon. Craig allowed the corporal to get thirty or forty yards ahead and then silently edged past the minefield that sealed off the mouth of the wadi and followed his leader, counting each stride as he went. Every now and then, Roberts would halt, turn round and wave. Craig would wave back and on they would go. On the surface of his mind, Craig was counting off the paces. Deeper down, he had that elemental feeling of being almost alone on the edge of the world. There were several thousand troops scattered around hundreds of square miles of hostile desert behind him, and God knew how many enemy troops ahead, massed for the attack. He and Roberts were the hinge between the two forces, he felt. It was frightening but exhilarating. Far better, he thought for the umpteenth time, than poring over clumps of letters and figures in some dusty room in the Home Counties.

The pace count soon passed the two hundred mark. Steady on, Shakesy, slow down. This is no time to chase medals. But just then Corporal Roberts halted, turned and waved both arms over his head, a signal for Craig to join him.

When he did, Roberts whispered, 'We're nicely in dead ground. And there's a natural little hollow just there that'll take the two of us. Give me a minute or two, then come quietly when I give the signal.'

The two of them had carried out more than half-a-dozen night recce patrols and had become quite a team. So there was no need for long explanations. Craig watched his leader wriggling into position, and when he saw the raised hand, he moved crouching into position alongside the corporal. The unceasing desert wind had chiselled out a saucer-like hollow and had banked up small sandy slopes that added to the illusion. Craig snuggled down. He took out the white paper pad from his shirt pocket, shielding it with his hand to prevent their precious position being betrayed to a watcher by a sudden flash of white. But the only activity to his west was a shooting star close to the horizon and, up above, a full moon, brilliant against the night sky.

On the other side of the low skyline, the enemy was less than quarter of a mile away. They could not be seen but, by God, they could be heard. Sounds travelled all the further in the desert at night but the noise made by the Afrika Korps would have assaulted the eardrums in the daytime as well. There were engines revving, gears grinding, occasional shouting and even a baritone chorus of Lili Marlene from a bored sentry. It seemed almost the revelry of a force expecting a quick victory. Craig hoped they would have a rude awakening when they advanced tomorrow morning, as they surely would.

Corporal Roberts began taking bearings on the larger sources of noise. Craig had turned his wrist-watch with the luminous dial onto the inside of his wrist so that no stranger would spot it. As Roberts whispered the numbers into his left ear, Craig wrote down the time and the bearing on single lines of his notepad. Experience had taught him that it is easy to write down numbers and even words in the dark as long as they were well spread out. And now, the brightness of the moon – a poacher's moon, they would have called it in Lincolnshire, Craig's home county – made night writing even easier.

Three-quarters of an hour went by. Craig reckoned that Shakesy Roberts had taken a bearing on every sound there was, even when the bored, unseen sentry let off a loud fart. Craig was getting stiff, just sitting on his haunches and taking notes like a bookie's runner. He had an idea.

Whispering softly, he said, 'How about this, corp.? If we move at right angles, say a hundred paces – that'd be on a bearing of three hundred and ten degrees – and took some more bearings from there, we could pinpoint the exact location of their tanks and guns. Where the two different bearings intersected. You with me?'

'With you, Private Craig, I'm way ahead of you. I'm thinking of tomorrow morning. What happens? They get in their fucking tanks and hitch up their guns and *move forward*. Get it? So what the fuck's the use of going back to

37

teacher and telling him stuff that'll be out of date in a few hours?'

Not for the first time, Craig received a sharp reminder that common sense is often more important than sheer brainpower. Army service was the liberal education he needed.

'Let's sum up what we *do* know,' the corporal continued. 'There's a large formation of tanks and mobile artillery right ahead of us. And they sound a bit cocky. They don't know we're as close as we are but, even so, you'd never expect crack troops – and they are crack troops – to make that much noise at night. They must reckon it's a walkover from now on. They...'

Craig nudged him sharply and put the other hand across his mouth. Silhouetted on the skyline, not fifty yards away, were three, no, four, Afrika Korps men, their helmeted heads against the moonlit background looking like black button mushrooms. One said something quite loudly and two of the others laughed. Neither Corporal Roberts nor Craig spoke German. Sudden movements, they knew, were all too conspicuous at night, so very slowly they eased onto their stomachs, then crossed their hands onto the sand and ever so gently lowered their bare heads onto their hands, face down. Knowing they would only be going halfway into no man's land and reckoning Jerry would not be patrolling at night, they had not bothered to black up their faces and the backs of their hands. But now in the betraying moonlight, the pallor of face or hands could easily give away their presence, unless carefully hidden.

Lying rigidly still, hardly daring to breathe, Craig could feel his heart pounding. He felt sure the thumping noise it was making would be heard by the enemy a stone's throw away. But the four apparently did not hear. They were laughing and jostling one another as they strode across the sandy ridges, crossing at a tangent in front of the Kent's observation post. Roberts and Craig did not dare raise their heads to look but they could hear disjointed bits of conversation and the swishing sound of boots on loose sand as they disappeared into the distance. The corporal eased round and watched them over the rim of the sandy saucer as they walked more or less due north, a hundred or so yards distant from the mouth of the wadi, and then looped back towards their own lines.

He waited till they disappeared into the dead ground near their starting point and then whispered to Craig. 'Doing the same job as us, I guess. Nice when you think you're winning, innit? That's the signal. Let's call it a night. You all right, Craig? Don't need to change your pants or anything?'

'Not this time, corp. But thanks for asking.'

Shakesy Roberts shook the sand off the compass and took a back bearing of forty degrees. There were two large camel-thorn bushes right by the opening of the wadi and he fixed his gaze on them. He followed the same procedure as on the outward journey; himself leading and Craig bringing up the rear fifty or more yards behind. Just short of the destination, he paused and waved to Craig to join him. They had not advanced ten yards when a voice challenged them. 'Halt! Who goes there?'

'Friend.'

'Advance, friend, and give the password.'

'Scorpion. Is that you, Dawson?' Roberts asked. 'I thought so. The noise you make. Anyone'd think you were back in Rochester Barracks.'

'Only doin' me job, corp.'

'Well, do it a bit quieter next time.' He and Craig eased their way past the small minefield and the sentry's outstretched rifle and fixed bayonet.

They reported to CSM Hogben, who was half-sitting, half-reclining on a sandy slope a few yards back from one of the forward sections. He did not interrupt the corporal's soft flow, which included the surprise appearance of the enemy's noisy patrol. Roberts ended with, 'Private Craig, sir, took notes of the bearings and the times. Would you like to see them?'

'No thanks, Corporal. I've got the general message. Lots of tanks and lots of guns just rarin' to go come daybreak. What did you make of that Jerry patrol?'

'Reckon their officer ordered them to swan around and check for defences in the area. An' they did a lousy job, sir. Too damn cocky. We'll show 'em.'

CSM Hogben thought: Jerry's far too cocky, reckons he owns the battlefield. Perhaps tomorrow he will. Out loud he said, 'I'll report back to the Major. Your information confirms the Long Range Desert Group's earlier report. I'll tell the CO you both did a good job out there tonight. Now you, Corporal Roberts, you go and get some sleep. We'll want you on your toes tomorrow morning. And it is almost tomorrow now, so move man! Craig, I want a word with you. Stay put here for a few minutes while I go and talk to Major Lapledge.'

He disappeared behind the narrow walls of the wadi. Craig sat down on the slope, wondering what all this could possibly be about. He couldn't remember doing anything particularly wrong, and in any case, that would entail a formal charge. What on earth would the Company Sergeant Major, in some ways the most powerful man in B Company, want to talk about informally, close on midnight in the middle of a battle? He thought and thought but could find no answer.

Five minutes later, CSM Hogben loomed over him, the bright moonlight casting a black shadow across the sitting soldier. He had been so wrapped up in thought, he had failed to pick out the quiet footsteps. 'Sir.' He began to scramble to his feet.

'Relax, man. You're not on parade.' The CSM sat down beside him. 'I won't keep you long. You need your beauty sleep too. Tell me something, Craig. I suspect you're an educated man. Am I right?'

'What do you mean, sir?'

'Ah, come on, man. Don't try to kid me. You're not exactly your average squaddie. Left school at fourteen and can hardly read or write. You passed your exam, didn't you? What do they call it? School certificate, right? Look, this is just between you and me, honest to God. You're not on a fucking charge!'

It was as if the CSM had pressed the confessional button. The words came tumbling out of Craig. Yes, he did get his School Certificate. And the High Certificate as well. And he had won a scholarship to Cambridge and was doing well in his exams when he was called up. But he had kept quiet because he didn't want the other squaddies to make fun of him.

'Right,' said 'Piggy' Hogben. 'Thanks for telling me. And it won't go any further, I promise. But when this little lot's over and we have time to draw breath, I'd like your permission to tell the Major and suggest he has a word with the adjutant. For you to join the Intelligence Section, I mean. They need guys with brains. You interested?'

'Yes, sir.'

'Right. I'll see what I can do.' He began to lever himself off the slope.

'Can I ask a question, sir? Where did I give myself away? And why me?'

'I make that two questions, Craig. It was that back bearing. You rattled off flat degrees in no time at all. Corporal Roberts is not all that slow on the uptake but he hadn't even begun to work out the answer when you came straight out with it. And why you? I don't want to preach a sermon but 1st Kents is my life. Oh sure, I've got a wife and a couple of kids, and I love them, of course I do, but I joined the regiment as a boy soldier twenty years back and it's been home and family to me ever since. We've had good officers and bad officers, good NCOs and bad NCOs, but slowly we keep on getting that bit better. And anything I can do to make things better still...

'You're a useful squaddie, Craig. I know that. But you'd be helping the battalion more – and yourself – in the Intelligence Section. That's all.'

Craig's mouth was dry and his eyes felt misty. On an impulse, he thrust out his hand. The CSM gripped it for a moment.

'And now bugger off to bed,' he said.

4

Dan Glenister had spent the past hour and a half walking to and fro in the soft sand, helping to site the back-up services, making sure the field-dressing station's tent did not project above the skyline, spreading out as widely as possible the reserve water and petrol cans and, above all, the metal boxes containing the spare ammunition clips. If they were too closely concentrated, a lucky hit from a mortar shell could send the lot up in one thumping whoosh, followed by a shower of lethal 'sparklers'.

Glenister took his time siting the latrines, followed by a bored sergeant and a press-ganged section of men. He knew from experience that the flies would be everywhere once the sun had warmed the air – buzzing in small swarms, alighting on any surface that held moisture, whether a mug of tea, the hot sweat pouring down a man's face or an open cut or graze. And having first harvested on the rich droppings of shit, they carried the filthy

45

contamination with them. A simple cut, unless covered up at once could quickly become a desert sore with its hard scab and thick pus underneath. Even after healing, the eventual scar and indentation would stay for life. Glenister had seen this happen too many times to risk it again, so he ordered the latrines to be dug deep, and insisted there was a plentiful supply of loose sand nearby.

They also had to prepare the two 'desert roses' – those ingenious contraptions made from old petrol cans beaten out with the hilt of a bayonet into a narrow cylinder with a wide funnel-like bowl on top. They were stuck upright in the sand. Men sweat enough in the desert, Dan well knew, but danger and the prospect of battle made them want to piss as well.

He stretched and yawned and thought back over the past few weeks. Although he had been called up on the outbreak of war, getting on for three years ago now, this was the first time he had actually commanded men in a battle. Because of his Territorial Army experience, he had been made a training officer at a large infantry recruiting depot where he had stayed for nearly a year. After Dunkirk and the likelihood of an invasion, he had been switched to help train the Home Guard. Over the next nine months, he made several requests for transfer to an active service unit in the Middle East, but it was not until Crete fell that he got his chance and even then, the convoy had taken two months dodging to and fro across the Atlantic, with a stop over in Cape Town before they reached Port Suez.

But he was to be thwarted still. Nicely acclimatised and raring to go, he had been called forward to join 1st Kents, only to discover he was to replace the battalion intelligence officer who had lost part of a foot on an anti-personnel mine. It was an interesting and responsible job, but not one he had been looking for. So when, a few weeks ago, B Company's second in command had been seriously wounded, he had pleaded with the CO to give him the chance. Which he did. Dan was gradually getting to know the men who counted, not least Major Lapledge, the commanding officer, a real mystery man.

Aching with tiredness, Dan took a last look around his area, reckoned that the smart troops were now fast asleep and decided to emulate them. He could just make out a sentry on the far side of the wadi mooching to and fro and yawning audibly. Half your luck, he thought. As he turned, he saw two figures approaching out of the inky shadows, and his hand automatically dropped to the holster of his Webley revolver. As they came nearer, he could see they were his company commander and the young gunner.

'Look what I've found,' said Roland, holding out a leather-bound flask. 'That idiot Billows, my batman, is not such an idiot after all. He filled it with Scotch from the Battalion HQ supply when no one was looking. Here, Dan, why don't the three of us – you, me and Jocelyn here – sit down, relax and have a swig?'

'My friends call me Joss,' said the young gunner.

'OK, Joss. Less of a mouthful. Dan, your turn first.'

Dan Glenister squatted down on the slope, feeling the sand give way under his weight. He took the flask and tipped it up. For a moment, he could feel the liquid burning his dry tongue and palate. As he swallowed, a drowsy warmth seemed to spread through his chest and along his arms. He breathed out slowly, wiped the screw-top of the flask on the back of his hand and passed it on to Joss Abbeyfield. When they had completed a second round of drinks and the flask felt more than half empty, Roland said, 'There's a game I like to play. Here we are, up in the blue, as they say, in the famous Western Desert. What the troops call, "miles and miles of shit-coloured fuck-all". It's near the end of June 1942. Think back three years. June 1939. What special moment stands out in your memory? Juniors first. Come on, Joss, out with the guilty secret.

Joss Abbeyfield hiccupped and then giggled. The scotch was at work. 'Easy,' he said, launching into what was clearly a favourite story. 'I had just completed my freshman year at King's College, Cambridge. King's, you know, the one with the famous chapel. What Ruskin called "the upturned sow." Rupert Brooke had been a scholar at King's. Christ, we actually believed that patriotic rubbish.' He struck a pose.

RICH DUST

'…Some corner of a foreign field
That is for ever England. There shall be
In that rich earth a richer dust concealed.'

He kicked up a jet of sand that spread into a silvery mist under the light of the moon. 'Rich dust, for Christ's sake! Miserable fucking stuff – nothing grows in it except bunches of reed grass and camel-thorn. He died guessing, did our Rupert.

'Where was I? Oh yes. My big moment that June was the college May ball. Sounds daft, I know, a May ball in June but that's the way it was. And very special it was, too. They hired one of the top dance bands from London, the men had to wear tails and the girls proper ballroom dresses. You dined and then the dancing began and it went on all night until daybreak. I had made up a foursome with my cousin Peter, who was at Cat's. I had rooms in college that year. Take note – this was very important! Peter's partner had a reputation for falling on her back without too much argument, so his plan was to leave the ball with her around half-past ten and go up to my rooms for a damn good screw. That would leave the coast clear for me, if things went the right way, to go up to the room with my own partner an hour or so later.

'Sophie, the girl I had invited, was a long-standing family friend. Up until our early teens, we had more or less grown up together. Then we had both gone off to our

49

different boarding schools and barely seen each other. We picked up again in the summer of '38. She had become one hell of a good looker – and passionate with it. The only snag was that her mother watched her like a hawk. My guess is that she'd been hot stuff in her youth too and knew exactly what her daughter would be feeling. Every single time we got down to any heavy kissing or groping and I thought my luck was in, Mum would come barging in on some lame pretext and I'd be left with a prick as hard and long as a twenty-five pounder straining my flies!

'But, God knows why, her mother actually agreed to her coming to the May ball as part of a foursome. Safety in numbers, I suppose. If only she knew! I had worked everything out with my cousin Peter beforehand. He had bought a packet of French letters from a chemist's shop off Market Square, and vowed he wouldn't use more than two at the most. The packet would then be left for me in the top drawer of my dressing table.

'Sophie and I were foxtrotting to Victor Sylvester's strict tempo. But we were more than dancing I can tell you – she kept rubbing her crotch against mine and left me in no doubt as to what was to follow. I could hardly wait, and neither could she. At the end of that dance, I caught sight of Peter across the floor of the marquees, and he gave me a nod, and a cheery wink. Coast clear – and no doubt as to what he'd just been doing! Just as we were about to slide off, Dadie Rylands, a don at King's with lovely wavy fair hair and a high-pitched voice, stopped for a chat. He didn't seem the type to be interested in women, though he was supposed to have had a long, drawn-out affair with a woman novelist, so I was rather surprised to see him chatting up Sophie. And downright annoyed – I had better things to do than talk to that bastard! At last, we made our escape. There were other couples strolling on the lawns, taking a breather. We mingled with them for a while, and then sauntered off. At the entrance to my staircase, I had a good look round to make sure a porter hadn't spotted us, and then we went up to my floor. I sported my oak to make sure we weren't interrupted – sorry, shut the outside door, that means – and then we shot into the bedroom tearing our clothes off the moment we got there.

'She lay back on the bed. I had never seen an adult woman naked before. I'll never forget what she looked like though... I could hardly get my underpants off with John Thomas at full stretch. I went over to my dressing table and pulled opened the top drawer. There was nothing there! I pulled out the socks and handkerchiefs and cuff links. Still nothing. I ransacked the other drawers at high speed. Not a trace of an FL! I sat down next to her. "Sophie," I said, "that bastard Peter's walked off with the French letters. What the hell are we going to do?"

'She looked at me, her face suddenly serious and said, "Joss, you're a good fellow and I like you, I really do. But we can't do it unprotected. You're too young to be a father

51

and I don't want to be a mother – not yet anyway." And then watching my prick still standing firm, she had a sudden fit of the giggles. That did the trick. Nothing like someone else laughing at you to make you lose an erection. For an instant, I thought she might suggest something else, lending a hand, you know what I mean? But she was too innocent to even think of it, and I could hardly suggest it, now could I? Anyway, looking down on my fallen member I reckoned it was too late anyway. So we dressed and went back to the ball and danced a few times to Victor Sylvester's "Forwards, one, two, sideways, one, two" and so on. I kissed her goodbye in the early morning; she went back to her hotel, and that's the last time we met.'

Major Lapledge pretended to brush away a tear, and then held out the whisky flask. 'That's a real tragedy,' he said. 'Here, Joss, have a swig.'

'Thank you, sir.'

'Enough of that "sir" stuff. We're off duty now. I'm Roland to you. God, what rotten luck! I hope you gave your cousin Peter a bollocking.'

'I bloody did, Roland.' Joss' voice was beginning to get a little slurred. 'He swore he'd left the rest of the packet in the top drawer as agreed. Apparently he went off to have a pee and when he got back, he noticed the girlfriend ferreting around in that top drawer. He reckoned she pinched the packet for use with another man. At least, that was his story.'

'Ah well,' Roland Lapledge said. 'That's really sad. Your turn now, Dan. I hope you're going to cheer us up.'

'Sure am, skipper!' He tipped up the now almost empty flask and took a swig before passing it on to Joss, who was still giggling quietly to himself. 'This was one of the high points of peacetime for me. But you need to know the background to understand it properly, so you'll have to bear with me, OK?'

Settling into position, he began, 'My father was a middle-grade civil servant, with quite a good salary. The idea was I would go to university – probably Cambridge, like Joss here – and become a schoolmaster. Then Dad fell ill, took early retirement and his income automatically halved. So no university for me, unless I could win a scholarship or an open exhibition. I tried two or three but the competition was too fierce – oh, most of them offered me a place but that would have meant paying full fees. Out of the question with the reduced income. So, on leaving school, I got a job with a bank instead.

'I had been a pretty good cricketer at school, winning the batting prize two years running. Not up to county standard but I might just have scraped a blue in a weak year, had I gone to Oxford or Cambridge. Anyway, I had a few games with Kent Club & Ground, virtually the county second eleven, in '38 and '39, where incidentally I met a very up-and-coming spin-bowler named Scrivener.'

'Not Private Scrivener, the bren-gunner?' asked Roland.

'The very same.'

'I'll tell you a funny story about him in a minute. But go on, Dan, sorry to butt in.'

'Where was I? Oh yes, cricket. Scrivener was really promising. Kent already had a long-established spin-bowler – indeed, a famous one – in Tich Freeman. Even so, young Scrivener got a few games with the county team in the summer of '39. Tich Freeman's a much older man, due to retire I'd say soon after the war and then Scrivener should walk into the team.

'But back to my story. A few miles south of Maidstone, where I worked, is a small village called Tovil. One of the branches of the Foster Clark family – you know, the jelly and drinks firm? – owns the local big house and a private cricket ground. They made up a home team largely from locals and then invited touring teams like the Free Foresters to play friendly matches. They'd got hold of my name from somewhere and invited me to play in a match starting the last Friday of June and finishing on the Saturday. Which meant having to get leave from the bank manager. But when he heard the details, he was all for it. I could tell what he was thinking – a few new, rich accounts wouldn't go amiss! There was to be a formal dinner on the Friday night and I had to hire a dinner jacket, stiff shirt and made-up bow tie. And they provided spare bedrooms in the big house for most members of the home team.

'I'd been at the bank for almost two years by then, and was bored stiff. Having to smile at customers all day long, and stamp the cheques and pay out a few pounds here and a few pounds there day after day, week after week – God, the futility of it all! If I come through this lot, I swear I'll never go back. Honest to God, I joined the TA out of boredom.

'So, when the weekend came, it was all the more of a thrill to mix with good cricketers in a luxurious background. The sun shone brightly all day long, there were pretty girls chatting in the deckchairs on either side of the pavilion and the wicket was as even as a billiard table.

'Oh, and I learned a lesson there as well. Before the game started, I was having some batting practice in the nets. There was an oldish man standing by. He looked a typical countryman, flat cap, red face, on the plump side and he spoke with a country burr. "Like me to send a few down, sir?" Humour the old fool, I thought. So I smiled and nodded. He walked back a few paces – he hadn't even taken his jacket off – and he came trundling in. His arm seemed to come over with a leisurely swing – I raised my bat to smash it out of sight, and the next thing I heard was a loud clatter as the ball slammed into the stumps. He bowled to me for five minutes or so, and I only managed to hit one ball, and then off the edge. As I left the nets, one of the spectators said to him, "You're in pretty good form, Arthur." He smiled and said, "Aye." "Who is he?" I asked the spectator quietly, as I went past. "Oh, didn't you know? That's Arthur Fielder. He gives coaching lessons to the boss' family."

'Arthur Fielder, Kent's great fast bowler who had retired a few years back. No wonder I couldn't get bat on ball with him bowling! And that's the lesson I learned. Never judge by appearances. In the last three years, I've met bright corporals and stupid generals. Take away the badges of rank – and where are you?'

'God knows, Dan,' Roland said, enjoying the tale. 'But enough of the sermon. Any more on your cricketing saga?'

'Yeah, just a couple of things. On a hot day – and boy, was it hot – after the first hour's play in the morning, the twelfth man usually brings on some lemonade for the players. Well, the butler from the big house came out onto the pitch with a silver salver and several bottles of champagne in a silver bucket! So this is how they live life in the upper bracket! I had never even tasted champagne before. The bubbles seemed to sing to me.

'Oh, and it got better! I scored fifty in the second innings and was applauded into the pavilion. Somehow I guessed that life after this was going to be all downhill.'

'That's a great story, thanks Dan. Hey, look, young Joss is almost asleep! We'll have to bottle you, Dan, as a cure for insomnia.'

'No, I'm not,' Joss Abbeyfield mumbled. 'I'm wide awake,' and gave a big yawn.

'I beg to differ, young Joss – and I'm the boss here. Go off and get some sleep. It could be a big day tomorrow.'

'What – and miss your special story?'

'It'll keep till tomorrow night. No, off you go. And if some keen sentry challenges you, remember the password's Scorpion – or you might get your own tail stung!'

Joss lurched to his feet and stumbled off into the night.

'He's a good chap,' Dan said after a moment. 'I was going to say "kid" but I guess he must be only three or four years younger than me.'

'Yeah. He looks so young. But he must be one helluva gunner officer. The RHA doesn't throw medals around. Here, let's have one last swig each, and then I'll tell my story.' They drank; Lapledge screwed the top back on the flask and settled back against the sloping sand on the side of the wadi.

'But first, my Private Scrivener story. It was before you joined the battalion, Dan. Must be nearly two years ago now. We were on embarkation leave and an uncle of mine, who happened to be an admiral, had invited me to dinner at the In and Out. The train was late getting me to Victoria and then I had to walk half the length of Piccadilly to reach the wretched club. So I ended up being about ten minutes late. My uncle was in the bar and I went over to apologise.

'And then I saw him – Scrivener, I mean. He was in RAF uniform, propping up the bar. With a squadron leader's rings and a fighter pilot's insignia, including a DFC ribbon! And, bugger me – he even had the top button of his service-dress jacket undone. Real fighter pilot style! He was holding forth in a posh accent to some captive brigadier on the merits of close air support. He must have spotted me but he never let on.

'I didn't know what to do. I was going to forget I'd ever seen him impersonating an officer, when my uncle saw me gazing at young Scriv. "You know that RAF fella?" he asked. "Real loudmouth, if you ask me." Like a fool, I told the old boy what I knew and asked his advice. "Clap him in irons," came the terse reply. So I had to report it when I got back to barracks, and Scrivener ended up with a month in the glasshouse. Dan, if I'm ever found dead with a bren-gun burst in my back, you'll know who the culprit is!'

He yawned and stretched. 'It's been a hell of a long day. Let's call it a night.'

'Come on,' Dan said. 'Fair's fair. You got us to confess our guilty secrets and now you want to bale out. No, sir.'

'All right. But I'll try to keep it short. This time three years back, 1st Kents were in Palestine. The mufti of Jerusalem was a Hitler fan and he was trying to stir up the locals against the British mandate. I was a junior officer with a detachment stationed in Haifa. A section down near the harbour is known as the German quarter, and quite a few Jews who hotfooted it out of Germany and Austria when Hitler came to power live there. One of them was a very old woman, said to be ninety, who was a soothsayer. One or two fellows in the mess had been to see her, more as a lark than anything, and had come away really impressed. They kept on at me till I agreed to go. I've always been completely cynical about astrology and tarot cards and crystal balls and all that nonsense. I reckoned it was just bullshit baffling brains.

'So when I did finally call on her, I was thinking, "Here we go again", especially when she asked to handle one of my possessions. Anyway, just to oblige I took my wristwatch off and she held it for a moment between her bony hands. She really was old, like a breathing mummy. She had a broken accent which I won't try to copy. I sat back in the darkened room, waiting for the usual guff. Then she said in a quiet matter-of-fact voice, "Your first name is Roland." At first, I thought, "Jesus, how did you know that?" and then realised any one of my friends could have easily told her beforehand. She passed her fingertips across the face of my watch and said, "You come from an old family in a foreign land." Now I began to feel just a bit scared. None of my mess mates knew that one of my ancestors had landed in England with William the Conqueror way back. *Laplage* – do you get it? *La plage –* *the beach* in French. King William had awarded the founder of the English branch with a chunk of the Kent coast and the local fishing rights.

59

'Then she said in that same broken voice, "One day you will read a story about another Roland, who died fighting for his king and country. He died because he was too proud to call for help. Soon you will be in another big war. History, they say, consists of repeating the same mistakes. Do not fall into that trap, Mr Roland." '

He went on, 'D'you know "The Song of Roland", Dan?'

'Only vaguely.'

'There wasn't a copy to be had in Haifa. At least, I couldn't find one in any of the local bookshops. Luckily, 1st Kents were repatriated when the balloon went up that September. We had a fortnight's leave and during that time I managed to get a copy from a bookshop off Oxford Street. The original long poem was in mediaeval French – way beyond me – but there was an English translation on the opposite pages. It's a terrific read, not least if you're a soldier. The gist of it is King Charlemagne has defeated the Moors in Spain but trouble has broken out back home, in what would now be Alsace-Lorraine. So he leaves a rearguard at Roncevaux, guarding the only real exit through the Pyrenees into France. He puts Roland in charge, with his great friend Oliver as second in command.

'Now Roland has a famous sword named Durendal and a battle horn that can be heard from miles away named Olifant. The Moors break the truce and attack the rearguard after Charlemagne has left with the bulk of his troops. But he is still well within range of the trumpet

60

Olifant. However, Roland wants all the honour and glory for himself and his "band of brothers", so when he does finally blow a dying blast, it is already too late – Oliver, his best friend, is dead and he himself is about to go down.'

'Great,' said Dan. 'What a delightful bedtime story! Thank God my other Christian name is George. First thing I do in the morning is check the radio transmitter's working. You can keep your Olifant!'

'You must admit it is a bit weird. We didn't volunteer for this lousy job. And how the hell did that old crone three years back know what was going to happen?'

'Search me, Roland. But I'm for a spot of shut-eye. See you at first light stand-to.'

Roland began to walk slowly and quietly back towards his forward post. The moon was still bright and, as it dipped, threw lengthening shadows along and across the wadi. He was still pondering the old crone in Haifa's remarks, as he had done half a dozen times since the CO's operation orders.

In the past two years of intermittent fighting he had come close to death on several occasions. A shell splinter had ripped through the roll-up of his shirtsleeve and had seriously wounded the man standing next to him. A bren carrier he had just left in order to carry out some reconnaissance on foot had blown up on a German Teller mine. Of the two occupants left on board, one had been killed outright by the blast and the other eventually had a leg amputated. And so on. Death, or its possibility, was a constant companion to troops in the desert.

But there had been no war on when the old crone gazed into the future with her weary eyelids. And how did she know his name was Roland? Or connect him with a rearguard action that was three years ahead? He liked things cut and dried, cause and effect clearly visible. This happening just didn't fit in properly.

His men were dug in on either bank of the wadi; in the quiet night, he could hear the even breathing of some of the closer sleepers. When he neared the main body, a drowsy sentry leaped to his feet and thrust out his rifle, then relaxed when he spotted his company commander. 'Night, Daniels,' Roland said. 'The enemy's more likely to approach from outside. You'd better be off keeping a watch that-a-way.'

He had sited his post well forward, about twenty-five yards in from the west opening of the wadi. His batman had scraped a shallow hole into which his rolled-out valise fitted. He reckoned that at this late hour the chance of an Afrika Korps night attack, never more than slim, was now out of the question. Oh, to get his boots off for the first time in well over two days! Then he noticed CSM Hogben sitting nearby with his knees drawn up.

Roland moved over and sat down alongside him. As he started to unroll the puttee around his right ankle, he said, 'Everything all right, Sarn't Major?'

'Well, yes and no, sir.'

'Let's take the yes bit first.'

'The men are all in place. Most of them are fast asleep. That faint light you can see coming from one of the rear slit trenches is Private Quested, sir. He's writing a letter to his wife back home. God knows if there'll be a runner to take it back to HQ tomorrow morning. Myself, I doubt it. But I gave him permission. It eases his mind. I hope that's all right with you, sir?'

'Oh, sure. And the no bit?'

CSM Hogben paused for a moment. They were speaking in barely more than whispers. The enemy was not all that far away. At last, 'Piggy' Hogben said, 'It's that Scrivener, sir.'

'Oh, Christ, what's he been up to now? Threatening to shoot me again?'

'Not this time.' Roland could see a flash of white teeth as the Sergeant-Major grinned. 'I reckon that was all a big joke when he left the glasshouse and rejoined the battalion.'

'Funny for some.'

'He's turned all nasty and edgy, sir. Take poor old Quested. A real farmer's boy, that one. He should never have joined the Army. Farming's a reserved occupation after all. You probably know, sir, that he went and got married on embarkation leave. And she sounds a real nice country girl. From somewhere near West Malling, same area as Quested. There's that story doing the rounds in the

63

battalion. You know the one, sir? A soldier in the Kents on duty in the desert hears through neighbours back home that his wife is going out with American soldiers. So he writes to her and says, "What have the Yanks got that I haven't got?" And she writes back, "Nothing – but they've got it here." Well, Quested's a peaceable fellow all right, but Scriv kept on teasing him until they nearly came to blows. Shakesy – Corporal Roberts – reported it to me. He more or less had to pull 'em apart. And another thing he told me is that Scrivener has been talking to his pals, telling 'em he's going to be killed tomorrow. Some are feeling jumpy enough as it is. They look up to Private Scrivener – bullshitter, crack shot, good cricketer and all that. When he tells 'em something, they're gonna believe it. An' if he's gonna get wiped, what about the fellas close by? See what I mean, sir?'

'I do. And I don't like it.' Roland thought for a moment. 'Tell you what, Sarn't Major. At dawn stand-to tomorrow, switch him to my command post and put another bren-gunner in up front. Tell him I certainly don't intend to be killed tomorrow so if he sticks near me, he'll be hunky-dory. I can direct his fire from the command post, and when I'm on the move, you can take over.'

'Right, sir.'

'One last slash and then it's beddy-byes. Rose of the desert, where art thou?'

'Piggy' Hogben pointed into the milky shadow where the tin contraption had a faint glint. Roland smiled his thanks, wished him good night and went to relieve his whisky-sodden bladder.

5

05.40 hours, 27 June 1942

Dan Glenister unhooked the top of his valise and shook his head, like a boxer at the end of a fight. A few yards away, Private Low, his batman and runner, was laboriously boiling water for a mug of tea on the desert stove, which consisted of a square petrol tin three-quarters filled with sand into which petrol had been poured, and the fumes lighted. It was basic but the small blue flames that flickered across the surface gave out heat intense enough to boil water in a mess tin or to fry slices of bully beef.

Water was always in short supply. The forward troops were rationed to two full water bottles, half a gallon, a day, all purposes. The Eighth Army's original water cans had leaked badly. They had eventually been forced to copy the enemy and have jerrycans with screw tops manufactured back in Egypt.

Dan picked up his right boot, banged it hard against a stone and then shook it, sole upwards. He repeated the drill with his left boot. Scorpions were known for liking dark hiding places and the residual warmth from a boot. It was bad enough having an operation code named Scorpion – he didn't intend to be stung by one as well.

His mind, never quick first thing in the morning even at the best of times, was still revolving slowly around Roland's strange story. He remembered now that when he moved from a spell at Brigade HQ to join 1st Kents, a gossipy officer named Peter Shaw had once told him that the Lapledge family owned a mansion near the village of Longfield. It had been in the family for centuries and was known as Beach House, although it was a good ten miles from the nearest beach. At the time, he had thought it a bit stupid, and dismissed it from his mind but now he understood the connection.

He poured a little water into his mess tin, wetted a clean rag and wiped it round his face and neck. Then he squeezed it out into the mess tin. Removing his razor, shaving brush and a chunk of shaving soap from his 'huzzif', he had a quick shave. The sun was not yet up and the chill water and the cold air made him feel alert, braced up for the day ahead. As if on cue, Low shambled forward and thrust a mug of hot tea into his hand. Dan took a swig. Christ Almighty, he thought, the little shit must have peed in this brew. It was rancid. But at least it warmed him. He tossed the dregs into the sand, said, 'Thanks a lot,' and went off to find his stand-to place.

Roland was up with the forward sections for the dawn alert. He could just make out the rim of the sun, almost as if painted with the thin edge of the brush, way back in the vast eastern stretch of the desert. Great, he thought. It'll be straight in Jerry's eyes if they advance in the morning. Which they are pretty well bound to do. Rommel is an attacker by nature.

Usually, at a dawn stand-to, there would be quite a bit of chit-chat and the gunners would warm up their brens by firing short bursts at made-up targets a few yards away. They would also seize the opportunity to entertain each other with the various tricks they'd picked up over the years. Roland recalled the one that only Scrivener could perform. He would set up two largish stones about three feet apart and perhaps twenty yards away. Then he would toss an empty bully-beef tin to land some ten yards short of the target. Selecting single action, he would fire one round after another, smashing into the sand just short of the tin, making it jump a foot or two towards the stones. The single shots almost blurred into one echoing fusillade, so quickly did he fire. Once he had jockeyed it into position between the stones but a foot or two short, he would switch to automatic and fire one sharp burst at the bottom of the tin. It would spin and jump through the 'goal posts' and land on the far side. To anyone who understood firearms, it was an extraordinary feat.

Indeed, one battalion wit had suggested that the GOC Eighth Army ought to challenge Rommel to a one-man competition – his best performer on a Spandau light machine-gun against Scrivener on his bren: loser to clear right out of North Afrika with all his troops and guns. A neat way to end a messy campaign!

Roland walked lightly across the soft sand to where Scrivener's section was standing to. As he approached he could hear snippets of that battalion favourite they were singing almost under their breath:

> 'I don't want to join the Army,
> I don't want to go to war,
> I'd rather hang around
> Piccadilly Underground,
> Living off the earnings of a high-born lady.
> Don't want a bayonet up me arse'ole,
> Don't want me bollocks shot away –
> No, I'd rather stay in England,
> Merry, merry England,
> Fuck, fuck, fucking me life away – gorblimey!
> Fuck, fuck, fucking me life away.'

Roland saw the others seemed in good spirits, but Scrivener's face was set, brooding, and he practically spat out the final words of the song. Roland had seen that look before – on the face of a soldier who had suddenly bolted from a front-line station, chucked his rifle to the ground and run blindly to the rear. In the so-called Great War, he would have been shot at dawn next day for cowardice. But in these enlightened days, Roland thought, they call it LMF – lack of moral fibre – and get the man chatted up by an Army 'trick cyclist'.

The last thing he wanted was for the best bren-gunner in the whole battalion to make a dash for it right in the midst of an enemy attack. When the stand-to had ended and the men were occupied with the serious business of getting breakfast – more mugs of tea and cooking up slices of bully beef to go on the hard, dry biscuits – Roland sought out CSM Hogben. 'I see our little problem is still with his old section. I thought you were going to shift him to cover the command post during dawn stand-to?' he said.

'I was, sir. But then I thought it might look suspicious. He's got eyes like a cat, that one. Could have seen us talking in the dark last night. So I reckoned to shift him now, sir, when I'm moving a number of the fellows around. Sorry if I've buggered it up, sir.'

'No, that's fine, Sarn't Major.' Roland thought, not for the first time, that the plump cross-eyed man in front of him was at least twice as bright as he was. Roland knew that 'Piggy' Hogden had left school at fourteen whilst he had stayed on and learnt which knife and fork to use and which glass to drink out of. Any justice and 'Piggy' would be running this company.

Roland moved around the forward sections, smiling a good morning at any who caught his gaze and mentally checking that the posts he had indicated in last night's darkness stood up to daylight scrutiny. One man from each section had been left in place as look-out. The others were milling around, preparing crude breakfasts on the petrol-soaked tins of sand or shaving or making sure that the treacherous sand dust had not infiltrated the mechanism of their Lee Enfield rifles while they slept. These were jobs that most of them had carried out several hundred times before and, he hoped, would survive to do them many hundreds of times in the future.

This thought reminded him. Private Scrivener had not been all that long in the desert, only just long enough to get his knees brown, as the saying went. And his month in the glasshouse for impersonating an officer while on embarkation leave had meant he'd missed the boat that carried 1st Kents to Egypt. He'd been left kicking his heels at the depot for some months until in the end he joined a detachment of First Reinforcements embarking for Middle-East Forces. These were the men held in reserve at a training camp in Amaryah, south of Cairo and close to the Suez Canal, and as casualties occurred among the troops up in the blue, fighting first the Italians and then the Afrika Korps, replacements were called up from the First Reinforcements. Scrivener had joined the battalion during a lull in the fighting a couple of months earlier. His first real experience of the 'sharp end' had come with Rommel's devastating blitzkrieg on a strung-out Eighth Army which had sent them reeling back to this present knife-edge situation. Perhaps it was no wonder, Roland thought, the young gunner was feeling twitchy.

He had a brief chat with a couple of corporals, one being Lakri Wood whom he had known back in pre-war days. He congratulated each in turn for well-dug and neatly-disposed slit trenches. Then he moved a few yards to the rear where Privates Scrivener and Quested were awaiting him. It suddenly dawned on him. Of course, every bren-gunner needs an assistant, to lie alongside him, slipping him a fresh magazine whenever the previous one was empty, even changing the barrel if it was getting too hot. The gunner could perform on his own but never so effectively. Quested was a slow shambling mover in ordinary life but he appeared to change gear when prone alongside the gun.

'You sent for us, sir?' Scrivener said. His tone bordered on the insolent.

'Yes. You will be responsible for defending the CP. I tell you what, you, Quested, I'd like you to go and collect up the spare ammunition. Then bring it here in relays. If there's time left over after that, you might care to dig one or two of these slit trenches a bit deeper. In your own interest. You could be using them shortly. All right?'

Quested nodded and slouched away. 'Now Scrivener, I want you to come to the top of the wadi, have a good look at the terrain and then decide where you're going to site your bren. This way.'

When the two of them were out of earshot, he asked quietly, 'What's this I hear about you saying you're going to be killed today?'

'Just a statement of fact, sir. Not against Section 40, is it, sir?' In the Army Act, Section 40 was the one that said, 'Conduct to the prejudice of good order and military discipline' was a punishable offence.

Roland said sharply, 'Don't fool with me, Scrivener. I was dealing with barrack-room lawyers when your mummy was still wiping your arse!' Not true of course but it sounded good. 'Statements likely to demoralise your fellow soldiers could indeed be an offence under Section 40. But forget that side of it – let's talk man to man. You're not the first to get the feeling you're for it. We all get that every now and then. But you've got to shake it off. Those predictions almost never come true. And that's why I've switched you to defending the command post. You'll be close to me almost all the time. I damn well don't intend to get killed today. Or any other day of this lousy war. You with me?'

The bren-gunner's eyes were darting to and fro, his mouth set in a downturn. 'Sorry, sir,' he said in a flat tone, as though trying to explain an obvious fact to a child. 'I understand you're trying to help. And thank you for that. But I've got this strong feeling, this premonition. It keeps telling me, "You're gonna get killed today, old son". Why would that be, sir, if it wasn't forecasting the truth?'

He wasn't being melodramatic, Roland could tell, just matter of fact, as if discussing the weather. Roland spent a few more minutes trying to jolly him along, stressing that defending the command post he would be far less in the danger zone than in his original position. 'I'm damn well going to see you survive,' he said. 'We need a man with your skills more than ever.'

Not for the first time an unpleasant possibility crossed Roland's mind. A soldier, threatened in his mind with death any minute, might suddenly cut and run back to supposed safety with the main body. And in a tense situation, others who saw him go might themselves turn and run, catching the epidemic of fear. Scrivener was a leading light in the company. He would be more likely than most to attract followers. Roland said slowly, emphasising each word. 'Let me make one thing absolutely clear.' He tapped the Smith & Wesson revolver in its holster on his belt. 'If any man in my company who thinks he might get killed once action is joined runs away from his post, I shall personally make sure the forecast comes true!'

For the first time that morning, Private Scrivener gave a grin. 'But wouldn't *that* be against Section 40, sir?'

In the desert under battlefield conditions, strange friendships develop. But, Roland thought, there was none stranger than the threesome of Scrivener, Quested and Groombridge. Scrivener tended to keep aloof, Quested hero-worshipped him and Groombridge, of all men, looked up to Quested. Quested was a countryman through and through. Big, broad, slow of movement and slow of speech, he was stolid and dependable. His passion, if such a calm temperament could ever be called passionate, lay in growing fruit, apples in particular.

Groombridge was his exact opposite. Short, dark, quick-moving, with a cockney fluency, he had walked the law like a tightrope. A spot of black marketing here, a few petrol coupons snitched from there, he had done his best to avoid call-up for the Forces. But when a police sergeant put a massive hand on his shoulder one day and told him he had two options – either Borstal where he might call in agony for release and not be heard, or the Army – he signed up, hoping to slip into a non-combatant unit, preferably stationed in or near London's East End. He was out of luck. As he said to a mate years later, 'If I'd been a few inches taller I'd 'ave finished up in the fuckin' Grenadiers.' His life for the next year was a running battle with authority, from corporals and sergeants to lieutenants, captains and majors until the truth of the old saying finally hit him. 'You can't beat the Army.' Once he got the message, his life was that much smoother, and, in a sense, happier.

A chance brew-up alongside Quested who was discussing the growing of black-heart cherries with another ex-smallholder who had ended up in 1st Kents, suddenly made Groombridge, the townie to whom nightfall was something dark and sinister, yearn for the open countryside. He listened to every word Quested had to say, parroted back to him the significant remarks and even began planning how to introduce a spot of 'oompah-pah' into their traditional ways.

And for his part Quested had found a keen pupil. After his talk with Scrivener, Roland had been on the point of moving away when some words of Quested's caught his attention. He stood in the background, listening.

Quested was explaining that different brands of apple come into season at different times. The astute fruit farmer can organise things such that the various crops will last for over six months. 'Lemme give you a f'rinstance. Take Beauty of Bath. Nice little red apple, juicy and sweet. I can have 'em ready for the shops by early July and they'll grow till the end of the month. Soon as they finish, up comes Worcester Pearmain, another good eater. By the time they're through, my Laxton Superbs are ready.' He pursed his lips and blew a kiss. 'Oom. What a taste. If the Good Lord said to me, "You can have one more apple to eat in this world. But only one. Take your pick," it'd have to be a Laxton. Then there's the Peasgood, great big yellow things weighing anything up to two pounds each. Far too big for the average customer. I had to dig it up in the end and plant a Cox there instead.'

'A Cox?'

'Yeah, Cox's Orange Pippin. Some very good judges reckon it's the best of the lot, but I'm not too sure. Give me a good Laxton and you can keep your Coxes. Matter of taste, I suppose. We get the early Coxes off to market in good time for Christmas. Nice sharp flavour about a Cox, specially when you've had turkey and Christmas pud. Cleans the mouth out, it does. My mother taught me a trick. Get a heap of old newspapers and some bushel baskets. Pick the last crop of Coxes, clean 'em up, make sure there are no bruised ones in the batch, and then wrap each one separately in newspaper. Fill the bushel baskets and hold 'em in with crossed pea sticks or the twigs from cobnut trees. They'll keep till Easter – and beyond.'

'What's a cobnut?'

'You Londoners are fucking ignorant, you know. It grows in the heavy Weald clay, bushes that never grow taller than a man, dark green leaves, clusters of sweet nuts ready for picking late November, early December. Far as I know, there's only about half a dozen of us growing cobs, because they need that special soil. There's the Beadles in Boughton Monchelsea an' a smallholder in Cranbrook. And one or two others.'

Groombridge said, 'So a few of you control the market. And I'll wager you sell 'em to the local grocer who gives you fuck-all for 'em. Wait till we get together after this little lot is over. I'll be flogging 'em to the Savoy and the Ritz for four times, maybe ten times, what you're getting now. Along with the Coxes and the – what was it? Laxton Superbs. Boy, oh boy!' He was almost rubbing his hands together at the prospect.

Roland smiled as he walked away. It was a weird conversation to be having with the enemy a few hundred yards away.

Lieutenant Johnnie Penfold closed his eyes and yawned deeply. He was tall, thin and his hair was the colour of ripe wheat. Being so fair-skinned, he hated the full daytime desert sun. If he rolled up his sleeves for any length of time, the blazing glare would turn his forearms a bright red. Blisters would then break out, and as soon as they dried up after dusting with the boracic powder supplied by the MO, further blisters would puff up from the shreds of the old ones. Night-time was his best time. No matter how quickly the temperature dropped, and chilliness stole down through the air, he would pull out his shirt and stand blissfully while the cold air soothed his sore arms and legs. It was risking CO's orders, perhaps even a court-martial, to catch a chill through disobeying the strict regulation to don sweaters as soon as darkness fell, but he felt the cool balm against his tortured skin was worth it.

He was chatting idly with Lance-Corporal 'Daffy' Norman. 'Between you and me, corporal, I can't see the point of standing to. You ever know the enemy put in a dawn attack?'

'No way, sir. But I've got a theory.'

Daffy was famous throughout the company, indeed the battalion, for his theories. The latest one was that Rommel had a twin brother who often took his place. The battalion had had some mail delivered a week ago before 'the balloon went up,' and Daffy had received a newspaper cutting showing Rommel with the Fuhrer at Berchtesgarden. The fact that the cutting was at least ten days old and that Rommel could have got back to North Africa by aircraft in a day did not deter Daffy. All the Krauts, generals or privates, stood to attention when Hitler spoke. Rommel was the flavour of the month, Hitler's current luck symbol, so Daffy argued, and it stood to reason that Hitler would be reluctant to let him go back. So it would have to be his twin brother who was running things on this side.

'So what's the famous theory this time?'

'This, Mr Penfold. I reckon this stand-to nonsense, if you'll excuse the expression, dates back to the Indian Mutiny. You know the Kents were mixed up in it? Right, I thought you did. Well, in those days there was no standing to at dawn. You just slept through till reveille woke you up. So the crafty *munts* crept through the lines, found everyone asleep in bed and cut their throats.'

'You know, corporal, for once you just might have something there. We love our traditions, don't we?'

'Do we not, sir. The cavalry were still prancing around on horseback up till a few years ago. They didn't get mechanised until the mid-thirties – and oh, what a fuss there was then. Some of the regulars who were with the battalion in Palestine pre-war told me when the order came through to drop the horses for tanks, a good few officers from cavalry regiments resigned. Went off to join the Trans-Jordan Frontier Force, which was going to stick to horses. And they weren't just the dyed-in-the-wool old 'uns. Most of 'em were young with careers in front of 'em. What a way to train for war!'

The stand-to had a few minutes to go. Dan Glenister left Company HQ and started strolling around the perimeter of the wadi's rear section, stopping here and there for a brief chat and the occasional question. He had quickly learned the hard lesson that an officer must be braver, stronger, more enduring, than his men. On the first twenty-mile route march after joining 1st Kents, he had ended up carrying two men's rifles in spite of a blistered left heel. In action though, it was usually easy enough for an officer to appear brave. On a night patrol, his mind would be fully occupied with questions – is the compass bearing accurate? Are we going round in circles? Is the supporting fire in position? What the hell was that password? But all the while the troops under his command had nothing to occupy their minds except the constant worry: 'does this fucking idiot know what the fuck he's doing?'

Usually, at stand-to, the men lolled around, yawning and scratching and holding their rifles loosely. But this morning he sensed a different note. They were more alert, on edge even. Several were lifting their rifles, removing the bolt and squinting up the barrels in the milky light to make sure the lands of the rifling were clean. Others had removed the ammunition clip and were working the bolt action to and fro; or adjusting the clips in their ammunition pouches to get them balanced and ready for quick removal. They knew there was a big day ahead.

Joss Abbeyfield's gun section had been sited behind the junction of the narrow strip of the wadi and the point where it widened out in an irregular circle. It had a fairly wide range of fire and excellent cover from all but direct hits. As Dan approached, Joss gave him a wave and a wide grin. He wore an off-colour shirt, a kerchief knotted around his throat, pale buff slacks and suede desert boots. His fair hair was tousled.

'Sleep well, Joss?'

'Like a baby, thanks. And you?'

'Yeah, fine thanks. How's your rich dust this morning?'

Joss waved an arm towards the latrines at the far side of the circle. 'All the richer – with a hundred men crapping their guts into it! Nothing like the thought of going into battle to keep your bowels nice and open.'

'Too damn right. At least, there's one good thing about being up in the blue – it takes your mind off sex. When we were pulled out for some R and R just outside Alexandria, you know Sister Street – *Rue des Soeurs* – every other house supposed to be a brothel, you needed an armed guard to keep the lads away. But drop them fifty miles or more from civilisation, put them on a survival course where the only female they ever see is a dead camel in a minefield and the only thing they think about is staying alive.'

'You don't sound too bothered by sex, Dan.'

'I should hope that's not true, long term. I do have a girlfriend. We got engaged on my embarkation leave. You know, Maidstone's really a small town at heart. Gossip spreads like wildfire. You're spotted kissing a girl – a perfectly innocent goodnight kiss at that – and the word is all round the town next morning. And working in a bank, you've got to be clean and sober off duty as well as on. I met Audrey, that's my girlfriend, at the local tennis club...'

'Thought you were a keen cricketer.'

'I am, but I play a spot of tennis, too. What was I saying? Oh yes, after Audrey and I had walked out a few times, her father took me to one side. He's a devout Baptist, by the way. He wanted a man-to-man talk, he said. It turned out to be a one-man lecture. He recalled the Great War.

Statistics proved that young infantry officers headed the list of fatalities. I was a young infantry officer, so the odds were right against me surviving the war. Now if I was selfish enough to rob his daughter of her most treasured possession – yeah, honest to God, those were his actual words – and then was foolish enough to stop the bullet with my name on it, Audrey would be committed to being an old maid for life. No decent God-fearing young man wanted "damaged goods," he said.

'I could hardly believe my ears. Women were there to be loved, I'd always believed, not traded to the right buyer. And there seemed a flaw in his argument. "Old maid" is short for "old maiden" – right? How do you continue being a maiden after being fucked a few dozen times?'

Joss chuckled. 'You've got a point there, Dan. So what happened after that?'

'The battalion was stationed at the Rochester depot, getting ready for embarkation. I used to get a lift to Maidstone once or twice a week and take Audrey to the pictures or to a meal at the Lyons Cornerhouse at the top of the high street. I'd then walk her back to the family home and give her a goodnight kiss. She's a nice girl and I have a hunch, if I come through this little lot and marry her, she's going to be quite a hot number in bed. That would certainly make up for the long delay! Or, of course, some rich Yank might get there first! Tell me something.

84

When are those Yankee bastards going to get out of bed – our beds – and start fighting this lousy war?'

'Too right, Dan. By the way, if it's not too delicate a question, can I ask what you make of Roland?'

Dan was surprised by the question. He paused. Then, 'Oh, he's a good man. I've known quite a few company commanders – he's the best yet. Straight and fair, that's all you can ask for.'

'You know his background?'

'A bit. I know, for instance, that he's the younger of two brothers. The elder one is an RAF fighter pilot, "missing in action". They don't add the next bit, "believed killed," but there hasn't been a trace of him since the Battle of Britain – what, well over a year back. Roland never talks about it. Too sensitive, I guess.'

'I have news for you,' Joss said. 'My sergeant, Billy Campbell is a natural born snob. Back home, the only books he ever read were *Debrett's Peerage* and *Burke's Landed Gentry*. He told me just now – literally ten minutes before you turned up – that Roland's father is a baronet, the fifteenth in the family. Sir Vernon Lapledge. Roland wasn't shooting a line with what you told me he said last night. His ancestor did arrive with William the Conqueror. He's got a younger sister but, of course, that doesn't count in keeping the family name going. Apparently, the father's pushing seventy and the mother's too old to have any more children.'

'So what you're saying is, if anything happens to Roland that's the end of the family line?'

'That's about it. So keep an eye on him, Dan, won't you? Don't let him do anything silly.'

6

07.50 hours, 27 June 1942

Roland called his O Group together in a corner of the wadi, twenty yards back from the opening. There were the three platoon commanders, Dan Glenister as his second in command, CSM Hogben, the bumptious Royal Engineers sergeant and Joss Abbeyfield.

Roland ran briefly through a repeat of the previous night's orders: total radio silence for the time being, and no firing until he gave the word. Having made sure everyone knew where the advanced dressing station tent was erected, he asked, 'Any questions?' and glanced around the group. 'No. Good. Now one last word. Oddly enough, the most difficult time is the next hour, hour and a half, or however long it takes for Rommel to put in an appearance. There's just damn all to do. You can't keep on doing rifle inspections. Somehow each of you has got to find the right balance. If you keep 'em on their toes all that time, it may be that they'll have lost the edge when the real moment comes. But on the other hand, if you let 'em relax too much now, they won't be alert enough if there is a surprise attack. So, chaps, try to keep it balanced. No last questions?'

As usual, Johnnie Penfold came up with the pointless question. 'When do you think they'll start, sir?'

'Christ knows! To be honest, I'm a little surprised things haven't hotted up already. Maybe they took more of a beating in the last few days than we realised. They could still be licking their wounds for all we know. Or they could come thundering over that ridge right now. Either way, we're stuck here till twenty-hundred hours,' he glanced at his wrist-watch, 'another twelve hours. Every minute that goes by gets us nearer close of play.'

Dan Glenister cut in. 'Do you want to stress the point, sir, about holding fire till you give the order?'

'Good thinking, Dan. Yeah, I should've mentioned this earlier. Part of the plan hinges on getting the lead tank to blow itself up in the entrance to the wadi. Just a few yards over there, gentleman. It's absolutely crucial we don't frighten it off by blasting away at long range. So make sure no bloody idiot in your mob thinks he's Al Capone.'

'One last question, sir.' It was, of course, Penfold, asking the unanswerable. 'The leading panzer comes along, goes up on the minefield with a bang. The crew open up the turret and come swarming out, hands up. What do we do?'

Roland opened his mouth, seemed about to say something and then paused. The silence grew. And in the silence Dan silently thought, that fucking idiot. Why bring it right out? He could have said nothing and then approached Roland privately for advice afterwards. But now it was out in the open.

To his credit, Roland did attempt to explain, 'I'll try to answer your question, Penfold. We are here to fight. We are under orders to hold this position for another twelve hours. We also have to provide a protective screen for the non-infantry types in this column – the sappers and the medical men. We have no spare men to guard prisoners or any stockade to put them in. You follow me?'

'May I make a point, sir?' It was CSM Hogben.

'Go ahead, Sarn't Major.'

'A couple of times when I was with the Second Battalion before Dunkirk, we would take up a defensive position. A German tank would blow up on a mine and out would come the Krauts with their hands up. One would even wave a white handkerchief in surrender. And as soon as we relaxed, one of 'em would reach behind his neck, pull out a grenade and chuck it at us! Or slip a Luger out of his thigh pocket and fire away. We lost a couple of good lads that way. We soon learned to shoot first – and sort things out afterwards. Same thing here, I reckon.

'The other thing I reckon, sir, is this. When that tank goes up on the mines, there'll be plenty of firing going on. If you're taking prisoners, someone will have to go out and collect them. That's risking men's lives unnecessarily in my book, sir. Besides, wandering about in front, they'll be spoiling the fields of fire for the rest of us, specially the gunners. What's the point of having a crack unit like the RHA helping you out, if you keep crossing their field of fire?'

Roland said, and Dan could sense the relief in his voice, 'Good point, Mr Hogben. Two good points, in fact. I couldn't have put it better myself. I hope that answers your question, Penfold.' Ouch, thought Dan, no *Mr* Penfold for him. He saw that Johnnie Penfold, too, had spotted the snub. The flaming sunburn on his cheeks went even redder.

'OK, men, that's it,' Roland said. 'Back to work. And good luck.'

Private Scrivener was tending to his beloved bren-gun. While his mate Quested sat on the side of the slit trench, his feet and legs dangling down its side, Scrivener was endlessly cleaning and probing. With the faintest skin of oil on his fingertips – too much oil would trap every particle of sand dust that shifted with each movement and breath of air – he made sure the catches that locked the magazine into place on the gun were working. Satisfied, he turned his attention to the bolt action, snapping it to and fro, sliding it into the cocked position and then releasing the trigger with a click. Quested, meanwhile, let his thoughts wander in the silence. His mind was on the smallholding between Snodland and Strood, west of the Medway. End of June –

the strawberry beds must be fruiting right now. He could picture his wife, Ethel, finishing the wash in the old copper boiler, wringing out the clothes with those strong fingers and wrists, and then, wiping her hands on the ever-present apron, walking over to the strawberry beds and stripping a line that was almost ripe, ready for tomorrow's market in Rochester or Chatham. Jesus, he wished he was there right now, not hanging around in this fucking awful sandy hell.

Corporal Shakesy Roberts came round the corner of the wadi and lay down alongside the bren-gunner. There were two thick tufts of camel-thorn protruding over the top of the wadi with a sufficient gap between them for a couple of heads to peer out towards the hostile western area. Shakesy had been tipped off by CSM Hogben to keep an eye on Scrivener. Only ten minutes earlier, he had yet again been heard muttering that he was 'going to die today.' It would have no effect on old Quested, Shakesy reasoned. The gunner's assistant was in a dream world all of his own. He hoped to Christ he'd wake up once the Afrika Korps arrived — even with a cork in the bottle situation, a hundred men would have their work cut out holding off an army.

Six months earlier, 1st Kents had been part of the division that joined the New Zealanders in inflicting a savage defeat on the Italian Ariete Division. The enemy had fled, leaving masses of stores and equipment behind.

At a junction of two tracks, the Kents had discovered a heap of largish cardboard boxes, piled one on top of another. They were curiously light. Torn open, they revealed scores, indeed hundreds, of condoms. Everyone present had grinned and laughed – there they were, surrounded by miles and miles of shit-coloured fuck-all, with not a woman within a fifty mile radius, and here were enough French letters to last a man a lifetime! It was not until several months later that anyone found out that the enemy had occasionally been supplied with 'military brothels'. Prostitutes would be flown in from the mainland and render services in a row of tents in a back area. To prevent venereal disease, commanding officers insisted that any Italian or German soldier visiting these girls use a condom.

The British, practical to the last, had used them for an entirely different purpose. Rolled over the muzzle of a rifle, a French letter would effectively keep the sand out. After a short while they perished and split in the fierce rays of the sun, but for that brief time they were useful.

For some reason Scrivener had hung on to his ration, using them sparingly and keeping the rest tucked behind his field-dressing pack in its special pocket. He still had one, distorted and stretched over the bren-gun's muzzle. It stayed in place as he rubbed the stock of the gun with a rolled-down shirtsleeve.

Shakesy decided on a joshing approach. 'You know what, Scriv? I reckon you love that bloody gun. The way you wipe it down. Looks like tossing yourself off. It's only a bit of wood and metal.'

'Yes, corporal. Thank you, corporal. You're the expert, corporal. If this bit of wood and metal shoots straight when Jerry attacks and knocks a few of 'em off, you may be quite thankful I looked after it properly. *Corporal.*'

'Oh come on, Scriv. Only a joke. Don't be so bloody serious. Let's change the subject. If you come through this little lot...'

'I won't.'

'Oh, forget the doom and gloom. You'll make it all right. Let's just assume you do come through. What are you going to do after the war?'

'Seems pretty pointless to me, even thinking about it. All right, I'll humour you. Two things. I'll go back to playing cricket, hopefully for the county. And I'll vote Labour.'

'Vote Labour? What about Churchill?'

'What about fucking Churchill? All he ever does is stick up two fingers and smoke big cigars. Half the chance, I'd stick up two fingers at him. We've done nothing but lose since he took over. Kicked out of France, kicked out of Greece, kicked out of Crete, chased all round the bloody desert by Rommel and co. You call that good leadership? Oh, and Singapore handed over to the Japs without a fight. Jesus!'

93

'We did win the Battle of Britain.'

'*We* didn't. It was the Raff. They saved us.'

'Which reminds me, Scriv. I've always wanted to know. What made you dress up as a squadron leader and ponce around the officers' club?'

'I'm glad you asked, Corp. I was testing a pet theory. It's the uniform, not the man that counts. Take your average upper-class pipsqueak. Been to the right school, knows which knife and fork to use but otherwise a total write-off. Put him in an officer's uniform, sprinkle a few pips and crowns around and, bingo, suddenly us squaddies are saying "Yessir, no sir, three bags full sir." Take our CSM. He can be a tough bastard but he's a man, a real man. But even he has to stand to attention with the jolly old "yessir, no sir," whenever the pipsqueak calls.

'Tell you one thing, Corp. I hired the uniform from that theatrical shop in Covent Garden. Then I walked down Shaftesbury Avenue and along Piccadilly. I knew I'd see quite a few sergeants on leave strolling about and window shopping. They all saluted the brave RAF pilot, who gave them a casual salute back. It grows on you. I almost tore a strip off one of them. I spotted him and he damn well spotted me, but turned away and looked into a shop window to avoid saluting. No, it's what I've been saying all along. Actually Burns said it much better: "The rank is but the guinea stamp"...'

'Now you've lost me, Scriv.'

'Hang on a mo. On CO's orders, I tried to explain it to the old boy but he wouldn't even give me the time of day. "Pretending to be an officer of another Service – in breach of Section 40 of the Army Act. Thirty days in the glasshouse. All right, Sergeant Major, march him out. Left, right, left, right. Next case?" No, apart from testing my theory, it was a gesture, let me tell you. My parents scrimped and scraped to send me to Rochester Grammar School. And I did pretty well there. Passed my School Certificate exams in seven subjects and, of course, played cricket for the school. We often challenged the King's School to a match but they were too windy. We'd have thrashed them, I can tell you.'

'The King's School?'

'Yeah, they're the so-called public school attached to the cathedral. With boarders in a big house the far side of the Vines, flouncing around in straw hats and, honest to Christ, walking sticks for the prefects! That was the first time I learned about "them" and "us". Their parents could afford to pay big school fees and boarding fees, so they were the salt of the earth. The rest of us were on the outside, looking in.

'I left school and played cricket as a junior professional with Kent Club and Ground, and the occasional game with the county. Same thing over again. Can you believe it? Kent had some great cricketers, men who played for

95

England and the MCC – Frank Woolley, Leslie Ames, Arthur Fagg, Tich Freeman. They were all pros. There were one or two good amateurs like Percy Chapman, the captain, and Mr B H Valentine – there I go, calling him mister! I wouldn't give you tuppence for most of the other amateurs. Oxford Blues, keeping an honest-to-God professional out of the team during what they called the Long Vacation. I'd give 'em long vacation – a full-time one.

'Every county cricket pavilion has two exits. One through the main part of the pavilion, where the members sit, and the other a side entrance leading straight onto the field. When a county team goes out to field, it's "them" and "us" all over again. The amateurs walk out from the pavilion with the members sitting there applauding. And the pros? They creep out from the side of the pavilion, straight onto the pitch, like a bunch of criminals. And if an amateur condescends to have a word with one of them, it's all 'Yessir, no sir, three bags full sir.' Think of it! Frank Woolley, probably the greatest left-hand bat who ever lived, calling some pipsqueak from Oxford "sir". Makes you want to spit!'

'When this lot's over, we'll find you a soapbox, Scriv, m'boy.'

'OK, Corporal, have a good laugh now. But you mark my words. Peace comes and all the forces'll vote Labour. You gotta have a dream. It'll be a new world with equal chances for all.'

'Pardon me while I brush away a fucking tear,' said Shakesy.

Dan Glenister patrolled his area for the umpteenth time. It didn't take a mind-reader to tell that the men were getting more and more restless. They were constantly readjusting their ammunition pouches, giving rifle barrels one last pull through, tightening webbing belts. He wondered, again for the umpteenth time, exactly what was holding the Afrika Korps back. Had they, as Roland had wondered, taken more of a beating than the Eighth Army imagined? Or had they advanced so swiftly they had outrun their supplies column? A man can't survive in the desert without water, nor a tank without petrol. Or perhaps it was the early morning sun, rising in the east behind the Scorpion defence and blazing right into the eyes of the attackers, putting them under a fierce spotlight once they broke cover, and dazzling their own forward vision. That was the real answer, Dan reckoned. Rommel was a thruster but he was too good a general to outrun his 'lines of communication'.

Dan strolled across to Joss Abbeyfield and his troop of twenty-five pounders. Joss was lolling back on a folding camp stool, one suede desert boot crossed over the other, as he read a book with crumpled covers.

'Boning up on Rupert Brooke, Joss?'

'The hell with Rupert Brooke! I wish I'd never mentioned that name. Him and his rich dust. Such a phoney! Wrote patriotic verse and probably never heard a shot fired in anger. No, this is the real thing. Listen...'
Adopting a pose with his right arm outstretched, he chanted:

> 'Cottleston, Cottleston, Cottleston Pie,
> A fly can't bird, but a bird can fly.
> Ask me a riddle and I reply:
> *Cottleston, Cottleston, Cottleston Pie.*'

'What's that from?'

'Oh Dan, you poor benighted creature! A A Milne. *Winnie-The-Pooh*. Wonderful stuff.'

'Yeah, I vaguely remember it. My mother read it to me once when I was a kid. Wasn't there an elephant mixed up in it somewhere?'

'Oh Dan, "tread softly because you tread on my dreams". Sorry, that's someone else. Yeats, I think. But let's not get too complicated. Milne had a son named Christopher Robin. The story is about a little boy of the same name whose toys, among them a teddy bear, Winnie, and a toy donkey, Eeyore, come to life and share the adventures. Problem is – small boys grow up. C R Milne was up at King's a little before me. They ragged him something rotten, it seems. He spent more time in the Great Court fountain than the local sparrows did.'

'Joss, how the hell can you stay so relaxed? All this waiting. I can't sit still a minute. Don't you ever get on edge?'

'Do I not? Underneath this pose, there's a heart beating furiously — like a virgin the first time she feels a hard cock up against her. Talking of which, my last leave I was burning up the town, and I used to go and see Bobby Howes' show and end up at the Four Hundred. Great days! And Bobby had that wonderful song.' In his light tenor, Joss sang:

> 'Here's a toast to the virgin sturgeon,
> The sturgeon is a very fine fish,
> Virgin sturgeon needs no urgin'
> That's why caviar is my dish.'

'D'you reckon those days will ever come back?'

Dan smiled as he walked away. Somehow he didn't believe Joss. The young man was too composed, too at ease to be feeling apprehensive. There he was, barely old enough to vote, a desert veteran who had seen it all and done it all and had a medal and bar to show for it. What a force he could be after the war, if he survived it.

The sun was rising steadily. Its rays were almost a physical force, relentlessly beating down on backs and necks. There were still some patches of shade under the steeper south slopes of the wadi that provided a welcome coolness for anyone stationed there, but those men sited to the north, gazing at the salt beds, had put on their goggles, secured with an elastic strap. All were in battle order with full equipment and wearing steel helmets pressing hard. The sweat rolled down their foreheads and into the lenses of the goggles, which misted up and required continual wiping and replacement. Sweat made dark blotches under the armpits and backs of shirts. When it dried under the force of the sun, a high tide mark of salt crystals remained. Most of the men had had a salt pill with their morning tea, which helped to replace the salt that had been sweated out. Now, with parched mouths and lips cracking with dryness, most would have given a month's pay for a long drink of cold clear water. Each had about a pint in his water bottle but that had to last until tomorrow morning. They all knew it would get much hotter and their thirst more severe in the next ten hours before the sun went down again.

Dan started one more futile tour of his area. Jesus, he was thinking, let's for Christ's sake get on with it. You spend most of your life in the Army waiting for something to happen and then, when it does, you miss the peace and quiet of the earlier phase. Come on, Rommel, stop fooling around, let's get on with it. But his rational mind told him that every minute spent now in this narrow wadi was a minute saved for the rest of the Eighth Army. They must be well on their way to El Alamein now. He could visualise all those tanks and gun batteries and soft-skinned trucks bumping along the coastal track or grinding their way across the desert. He remembered the western extremes of Egypt were relatively flat and hard with scattered boulders. A fifteen-hundred weight truck might speed up to twenty miles an hour in that area. Good luck, he thought – and good luck to us, too.

It was a nasty job in the heat of the sun but he felt he ought to inspect the latrines and make sure the men were shovelling plenty of sand over their droppings. The canvas strip that afforded some privacy was held up by two poles, one at either end. Already, a dark cluster of flies was buzzing close to the nearest one.

When he was a few feet away from the entrance, he heard a noise like ripping calico, followed by what sounded like a groan. He strode through the gap. He saw Private Timmins squatting, shorts around his ankles, his rifle and equipment flung wildly in front of him and a look of abject misery on his face. He tried to struggle up when he saw his second in command but Dan cut in.

'At ease, Timmins. Are you all right?'

Timmins was only just eighteen years of age. He had volunteered at sixteen and had lied about his date of birth. As he was tall for his age, an inch over six foot, the recruiting sergeant had winked and passed him through. He had reached Egypt three months before as First Reinforcements to the Kents and had been in the desert now for over a month. Slim as a youth, he was now gaunt.

'I'm sorry, sir. It's this bloody dysentery.'

'Oh God, what awful luck. At a time like this.' Apart from the general smell that pervaded the latrines on this still day, Dan could detect an acrid stench in the area where Timmins crouched. 'Bloody dysentery' might be an apt description. With amoebic dysentery there would be a regular discharge of blood. But this, he felt, from the symptoms, was more likely to be bacillary dysentery. Even so, he knew from his own experience soon after arriving in the desert that the explosive outrush occurring perhaps ten times a day, soon made the rectum sore and internal bleeding could result.

'I can't help it, sir,' said Timmins woefully. 'The others laugh and joke and say I'm shit scared. That's what makes me keep running to the lav, they say. But that's not it, sir. It's the dysentery. One moment, I'm fine, right as rain. Then there's this awful corkscrewing pain – an' if I don't rush to the lav there and then, I'd be shitting in my pants, if you'll excuse the expression.'

'I do understand. Tell you what. When you've finished there and cleaned up, go along to the medical station. Tell 'em I sent you. They may have a pill or something that would help your condition. And again, tell 'em from me, they are to give you half a pint of cold water out of their stocks. I know how dysentery dries out the whole system. We've got a big job to do today.'

7

And still they waited. The sun had become a burden. Soaring ever higher in a cloudless sky, it shone down on the defenders with ferocious force. The temperature in the shade, or what little shade there was, had risen steadily through the nineties and was now in the low hundreds. Anyone who so much as touched a piece of metal exposed to its relentless rays, would jerk his hand back instantly. The metal was simply too hot to hold.

The sun had drained the overhead sky to a blanched whiteness but to the north, over the Mediterranean, it was still a darkish blue, reflecting the colours of the inland sea. The platoon on that flank were wearing their goggles, but even so the blinding dazzle of the salt pans forced them to look down at their own sweaty shadows every few minutes, close their eyes and wait till they could see clearly again.

Roland elbowed his way up the wadi's slope, beckoned Quested to move over and took up a position alongside

103

Scrivener and his beloved bren-gun. The private gave a grunt, which might have meant 'Good morning, sir. And how are you on this fine morning, sir?' or might equally have meant, 'Fuck me, here's another cunt blocking my view. Why don't you just fuck off – sir?' Roland, drawing out his field glasses, which had been sandblasted to avoid dazzle, would have bet heavily on the latter.

Although it seemed too early in the day, with the naked eye he could see mirages at the far end where the track disappeared from sight. They were like narrow lakes on either side of the track, calm and refreshing. As he kept on looking, he could almost detect a ripple on the surface of one. God, what a bloody place to fight a bloody war. For an instant he remembered the pond at Beach House, where he had often swum as a boy, the peaty brown cold water, the solitude. Roll on demob! Except there would be no demob for him. A regular soldier served on, peace or war.

Dan, part-way through his trip around the whole wadi, came up and crouched on the sloping bank. 'Any activity?'

'Not a whisper. Dead as the grave – forgive the expression – out there.'

'I've got a new theory. I think Rommel's playing a crafty one. He's going to do nothing and bore us all to sleep. Then he and his boys will come tiptoeing past and get on with the Alamein gallop.'

'Clever stuff, Dan. You ought to be back on the staff!'

Ignoring the two officers, Scrivener was mumbling something to himself over and over. Dan thought it a weird kind of incantation and wondered whether the heat and the tense expectation of battle had finally got to the bren-gunner. He, too, had heard the rumour that Scrivener was threatening to die that very day. Was he about to snap and do something suicidal? And why was Roland, usually a perceptive commander, doing nothing about it? He rolled on his side and said in a low voice, 'What's he up to?'

'He's saying over and over, "Johnnie, get your gun."'

'"Johnnie, get your gun?" What the hell's all that about?'

'Simple. Back in peacetime, I did a bren-gun course at the School of Musketry, so I know the secret. There's always a risk with the bren of ripping off a whole magazine in one burst. Specially when it's nicely warmed up. The plan is to fire short bursts and save ammunition. You see, a bren-gun fires a very concentrated burst, not the scatter effect of a shotgun. An ace like Scrivener could blow the bull's eye out of a target with a longish burst. You don't need twenty or thirty rounds to kill a man. Not if you hit him fair and square in the chest. One or two will be enough.

'But how do you make sure? You can't count the rounds away, they go too quick. So they had to come up with a code to tell the gunner when to take his finger off the trigger. That's how "Johnnie" was born. If you pull the trigger, say

105

to yourself at normal speed, "Johnnie, get your gun" and
then release the trigger, on average you will have fired a
burst of four or five rounds. Just right. Now, young Mr S
hasn't fired his pet gun for a couple of days so he's making
sure he's back in the groove.' Roland paused, and said with
a smile, 'Any time you want to learn about the Army, Dan,
just stick around!'

As Dan was scrambling back down the slope, Scrivener
said in a calm tone, looking sideways at his company
commander, 'I think there's something beginning to
happen, sir.'

Roland slowly raised his binoculars. From the reverse
slope some four hundred yards away, a German tank
trundled into view. It paused and its seventy-five-
millimetre gun swung slowly through an arc of over ninety
degrees, searching for its enemy. From that range, it looked
like some miniature prehistoric monster risen from the
swamps. It crept forward fifty yards and then paused again.
Once more, the long gun swung to and fro. At last, satisfied
there was nothing hostile lurking up ahead, it cruised
onwards. Other tanks followed in line astern, fifty yards
apart.

Roland leaped up and moved round the forward
sections, saying, 'Hold fire! Fingers off triggers! I say
again, hold fire!' He was glad to see Company Sergeant
Major Hogben working his way quickly down the south

side of the wadi, warning the men to be alert but not to open fire.

The leading tank came closer. As the turret swung slowly from side to side, alert for the flash of sun on metal, the defenders could now spot its insignia, stencilled on both sides, with the naked eye. It was the 15th Panzer Division all right, one of the best of Rommel's tank *gruppen*. Behind it, other tanks fanned out until those on the north encountered the edge of the salt flats and those on the south the steep escarpment deflecting their drive. One by one, they returned to single file behind the leader, now less than fifty yards from the wadi's opening.

Roland found himself holding his breath as the giant machine loomed closer, almost blanking out the daylight. 'Come on, for Christ's sake, come on,' he was urging it in his mind. 'Hit those fucking mines.' It seemed almost within touching range. The barrel of its seventy-five-millimetre gun was about to penetrate the narrow opening. He heard the snick of a rifle bolt away to his right. 'Hold it,' he shouted, reckoning his voice would not be heard inside the tank with its lid down and tracks churning towards the trap. 'Do – not – fire. I say again, do – not – fire.'

A sudden chill went through his bones. What if the EP mines didn't work? The leading tank would then come rumbling along the path and into the wadi, its machine-guns blasting away at any opposition. And all the other tanks would grind along in a single file with the infantry personnel carriers wedged safely between them. On they would go, leaving B Company's survivors to be put in the bag at the Afrika Korps' leisure. And black disgrace for the company commander who had let them straight through without a fight.

But the EP mines did work. There was a resounding crash, a blast of fine sand shooting upwards and sideways, and the lead tank lurched sideways, its offside track smashed into fragments. Fifteen, twenty seconds passed and then the turret lid was pushed back and a figure started climbing out, followed by another. With the lid open, Roland could hear a man groaning somewhere inside the tank. Anyone sitting on that side would have felt the full force of the blast.

His natural instinct was to send a couple of his own troops to climb into the panzer and get the casualty out. But that would give away the fact that British troops were manning the wadi. And the enemy machine-guns would almost certainly open up at the mercy mission. Something had to be done about the two German tank crew climbing down to the ground, and done quickly.

Something was done. Scrivener swung his bren-gun to one side and fired two short bursts. The impact forced one of the men back against the bottom of the turret before sliding down the sloping side. The other, like a broken doll, just fell limply to the ground. Both were dead before they

108

hit the sand. Roland, his ears crackling and his head buzzing with the noise of the bursts a few inches from his left ear, didn't know whether to curse young Scrivener for giving the game away or to congratulate him on such accurate shooting. So he did neither but stood up in the open and gave Joss Abbeyfield the pre-arranged hand signal for the RHA to select their own targets and open fire.

The twenty-five pounder gun had been designed for long-range firing. The Royal Artillery detachments were therefore usually stationed several thousand yards to the rear of an action. But the more mobile Royal Horse Artillery had learned to fire their twenty-five pounders over open sights directly at enemy tanks, using armour-piercing shells. Whereas with long range firing, the shell's passing, high in the sky, made a keening sound, shells aimed at a target close to the ground made a fierce rumbling as they burst the air aside. Pressing your head against the unresisting sand and putting the palms of your hands over your ears was the only way to keep out the blast.

Roland watched with surprise and growing admiration as the gunners fired. A nearby tank, perhaps a hundred yards away, was hit twice. It swivelled to one side and black, oily smoke, went up in a leisurely spiral. Another tank, fifty or more yards further away, burst into flames. A third started to move in a small circle – obviously

'wounded' in one of its tracks until a further well-aimed
shot halted it for good.

Putting his binoculars down, Roland could hear Shakesy
Roberts muttering, 'Every time a fucking coconut.' Too
right, he said to himself. Thank God they're on our side.

The panzers that had not been hit backed off and
zigzagged back into the dead ground that had hidden them
from B Company. A silent minute went by. Roland,
crouching close to the leading defence section, straightened
up and did a quick tour round his leading troops. He
looked back and saw Joss Abbeyfield lolling against the side
of one of his self-propelled guns. He waved and held up his
thumb in salute. Joss waved back.

CSM Hogben approached. 'That fella in the tank's
stopped moaning, sir.'

'So he has, Sarn't Major. You reckon he's had it?'

'Could be, sir.'

'You feel we ought to find out?'

The CSM shook his head briskly. 'No way, sir. They
could have a sniper or two under cover out there, just
looking for trouble. We send a couple of good men into that
tank to get the fella out, and they cop it when they lug him
out and onto the ground? No, sir, I'd leave him for now.'

'Anything else, Sarn't Major?'

'Those two fellas Scrivener got, sir. It wouldn't be
breaking cover to retrieve those bodies and leave 'em back
there near the dressing station. One or two of our lads up

front might be a bit squeamish, sir. The leading troops are barely six feet away from 'em right now.'

'Good thinking. Right, Mr Hogben, would you go back to Captain Glenister and ask him if he would provide a couple of stretcher teams to come forward and remove the dead krauts. It's up to him but, personally, I don't think they should be buried. Just laid out neatly. So when the Afrika Korps does finally come through the wadi, they'll find those two and any others we bag with their identity discs and so forth. All right?'

CSM Hogben sketched a salute and strode off towards the rear section of the wadi. As he watched his retreating back, Roland wondered what the hell he would do without him. The man was good sense personified.

Private Quested cut into this reverie with a shout. 'They're coming again, sir!'

Roland snatched up his binoculars. Four or five hundred yards away, a line of men four or five yards apart trotted forward about twenty yards and then fell to the ground. As they did so, another extended line to their left, who had thus far been concealed, leaped up and trotted forwards. Then the first line opened fire with rifles and Spandau light machine-guns. In the clear desert air, the high-pitched rattle of the Spandaus sounded exactly like the noise a young boy makes running a stick along a set of railings. But here the results were more deadly. Some of the rounds fired went screaming over the heads of the defending troops, the split air making a noise like a series of whip cracks. Several rounds ricocheted off the damaged tank at the mouth of the wadi. One dipped and, spinning sideways, gouged a chunk of flesh out of the upper arm of a soldier in Lieutenant Penfold's section. 'Hell, our first casualty,' Roland murmured to himself, crouched a few yards away. 'He's a young, fair-haired bloke. Now, what the hell's his name? – Willis, Wilson? – yes, that's it, Willis. Now let's see if Penfold's as good with the deeds as he is with the words.'

Private Willis pulled his field-dressing out of its enclosure with his good hand and slapped it against the open wound which was still spewing a steady stream of blood. Penfold had moved quite fast. He had sent a runner back to the rear echelon and within a couple of minutes an RAMC orderly had come forward, carrying a medical bag. On hands and knees, for the Afrika Korps bullets were still blasting in, he disinfected Private Willis' wound, bound it up and, carrying the wounded man's rifle, helped him back to the field-dressing station for more attention.

By now the German infantry were about three hundred yards away. Their approach was almost like a parade ground demonstration, one half moving forward at a steady pace while the other half gave them covering fire. They had to be stopped – fast.

Bent low, Roland moved a couple of paces to his left. He called out, 'Scrivener, Quested!'

'Sir.'

'Target to your right. Two-hundred yards. Take out the enemy when he is upright and advancing. I say again, upright and advancing. Go!'

Quested shuffled a couple of full magazines towards the other man's left hand, while Scrivener was swivelling his bren-gun into position to the right. He turned the switch to 'single action'. Then Roland, gazing through his binoculars, saw a class of accurate shooting he would never forget, however long he lived. As the half of the enemy who had been giving supporting fire, rose to their feet, he heard *crack,* pause, *crack,* pause and so on, each single round fired every two to three seconds. And through his binoculars, Roland saw one man after another, face contorted, stop as though he had walked straight into a brick wall in the dark and then fall flat, dead. Only one of them survived, and only because he had happened to stumble just as Scrivener fired at him. Roland reckoned he must have been hit in the upper arm, judging by the fact that he dropped his rifle and clutched a place above the elbow with his left hand. The other advancing Afrika Korps men, seeing what was happening, chose discretion and dived for cover.

'OK, Scrivener, cease fire,' Roland said in a half shout. 'Fantastic shooting! You win the cigar. When we go back on R and R, you come and remind me and I'll buy you the best cigar in the whole of Alex.'

'Nice of you, sir, but there are two things against that. One, I don't smoke; two, I reckon to be killed today. Sir.'

'To which I reply, with all credit to a great artist with the bren – bollocks!'

Shakesy Roberts was peering out from behind a convenient bunch of camel-thorn on the top left edge of the wadi. 'Movement ahead, sir,' he called. 'Take a shufti with the field glasses.'

Roland adjusted the range wheel in the middle until the focus was correct. That Shakesy must have an eye like a hawk, he thought. Even with the binoculars, he could only just discern the prone bodies wriggling in an erratic line around to the north side. Right towards the salt pans, dazzlingly brilliant in the midday sun.

The leading troops reached the edge. Not realising the horrors they were about to encounter, they crept forward, cracking through the crust of salt into the six inches or so of black slime underneath. They paused. Two or three of the more determined plunged on, enveloped in the dark goo. They could hardly move, forwards or backwards. Lieutenant Penfold's section on the north side of the wadi opened fire, killing at least two and wounding several others. Even so, the rest did not falter or lose discipline but wriggled their way back to the dead ground and safety. Roland, watching them through his binoculars, felt fairly certain they were part of the 90th Light Division – crack troops in what was a good fighting force, the Afrika Korps.

114

The firing stopped. There was a moment of blessed silence, and then a minute or two. Five minutes went by and still nothing happened. Roland, suddenly feeling a little weary, sat back against the slope of the wadi side, removed his steel helmet and wiped his forehead and neck, streaming with sweat. The time had fled past. It was already mid-morning. So, one way or another, we've seen off their first attack, he thought. Of course, there'll be another — several, in fact. Rommel's just got to make the track through the wadi usable for his tanks and trucks. And it's up to us to keep them out for — what? Another eight hours, nine perhaps.

He moved round the forward sections, telling the platoon commanders to stand down half their men in turn for a brew-up and a snack of corned beef and a hard biscuit. He reckoned it would take the enemy at least an hour to lick his wounds and prepare another attack, so they might as well make best use of the time. He then went back to see how Dan Glenister and the rear echelon were faring.

On his way back, he had to pass the RHA detachment. Joss Abbeyfield, bareheaded, sprang to an exaggerated attention, head up, chin in, chest out, hands clenched and thumbs pointing down the seams of the trousers.

'Fantastic shooting, Mr Abbeyfield,' said Roland.

'We aim to please,' he paused, 'sir.'

'All right, Joss. Relax, man. This isn't CO's inspection. Fooling apart, that was something special. I've seen quite a bit of gunnery all these months up in the blue. But nothing to beat that performance.'

'Don't thank me, sir. I'm only the officer in charge. It's Sergeant Campbell here and his men who deserve the praise, not me.'

There was not a spare ounce of fat on Sergeant Campbell's body. He was hard, sinewy, with nut-brown arms protruding from his rolled-up shirtsleeves. He looked at Joss, 'Leave to speak, sir, please,' and, without waiting for permission, carried straight on with, 'that's complete bullshit, sir. Mr Abbeyfield's a crack shot over open sights, as good as any of us troopers. And if we're good – and I reckon we are – it's because he trained us. Nothing sloppy gets past him, sir.'

'Sergeant, you're making me blush,' said Joss.

'That'll be the day, sir,' the sergeant grinned.

From their feats of shooting when the panzers first appeared and the easy banter he had just witnessed, Roland knew this was a crack unit. Once again, he felt himself lucky to have them assigned to Operation Scorpion.

'Thanks for all the good work, Joss,' he said. 'I'm off to have a word with Captain Glenister. You'll keep the chaps on their toes, won't you? We may have knocked that first probe back but they'll come again. They've got to.'

'You bet, skipper. You bet.'

When Roland reached the point where the wadi widened out, he could see Dan in the distance talking to the RAMC sergeant in charge of the advance dressing station. He waved. Dan broke off talking to the sergeant and began to walk towards him. Neither saw the small dot in the sky a mile or so to the east. They had not considered the possibility of enemy action from what, logically, was a safe area.

The dot rapidly grew bigger and bigger as it tipped into an almost vertical dive. The accompanying howling scream almost blasted their eardrums. It was a Stuka, a German dive bomber, fitted with a device on each wing that used the air rushing past to make the chilling noise.

Roland and Dan dived for the nearest trench. They knew from experience that the blast from its bombs would be trapped in the narrow confines of the wadi. In a previous Stuka attack, Roland had seen a man's head blown clean off his shoulders as the unfortunate soldier looked up above his slit trench to see what the noise was. But this time the Stuka dropped no bombs. Levelling out about fifty feet overhead, it flew along the whole length of the wadi and, climbing, soared away towards the German lines. There were a few ragged volleys from the troops up front but the Stuka sailed on and finally disappeared.

Roland had been first to dive into the nearest vacant slit trench and Dan had landed on top of him. They heaved themselves out and began knocking the sand out of their ears and off the backs of their necks and bare knees.

'You do that once more, Dan, and you'll have to marry me!'

'Ha-bloody-ha. What do you make of that? Had he run out of bombs, you reckon?'

'No way. He wasn't on a bombing sortie, that's for sure. No, it was simply reconnaissance. Right now, he'll be reporting back on the R/T, telling the boys on the ground what they're up against. Or how few they're up against. And he's probably got the films to prove it.'

'You sure?'

'Think about it, Dan. That Stuka was never going to bomb us. Why? Because 15 Panzer and 90 Light have got to use the track when we move out. They'll want to come through like shit off a shovel, not spend hours filling in holes and brushing away tons of sand. You get it?'

'Yeah. That makes sense.'

'What's the position with casualties?'

'Four or five wounded. Mostly ricochets from the Spandau fire. One quite serious. He ought to be sent back on the first vehicle out. The others have been patched up and sent back to their units. Oh, and there's one poor soul suffering from heat exhaustion.'

'Is he skiving?'

'No, it's genuine. He's a good soldier, Private Timmins. He's had the most terrible attack of dysentery, poor kid. It's drained him dry.'

'You've got a platoon from our company dug in back here, Dan. Keep 'em on their toes, won't you? The krauts could be back any minute.'

8

14.35 hours, 27 June 1942

But they weren't. Midday dragged on into early afternoon. The men in B Company ran their parched tongues over lips cracked with thirst and apprehension. They had used half their daily water ration in the morning and midday brew-ups. There would be no more tipping up of water bottles until the gradual cool of early evening.

There was very little shade inside the wadi against the baking glare of the sun. As it moved slowly from south to south-west, those stationed on the southern slopes of the wadi found themselves to be the lucky ones with emerging pools of shade. But those on the north side had the worst job, feeling the heat and pressure of the sun on their backs and necks while they were almost blinded by the fierce dazzle of the salt flats straight in front of them.

The only event to break the monotony was the passing of a sand devil. Somehow the rising heat from the sun had hit a layer of cooler air drifting down from the Mediterranean.

The resulting sand devil had twisted and spiralled until it reached ground level, gathering up dust and sand and quickly becoming a mobile spinning column. It drifted eastwards, almost keeping to the track that ran up to and through the wadi. The men could do nothing except grab their groundsheets and cover their weapons and their heads while the seething, choking, whirling cloud of sand lazily moved past. Those who had been unable to take cover were left sneezing and coughing, having to spit out the sand particles through dry lips. It took several minutes for order to be restored, and for the men to be alert and back in position.

My God, Roland thought, we were lucky. If the Afrika Korps had had even half a battalion ready to move, they could have advanced behind the screen of the dust devil and taken us there and then. Christ, what an escape.

He moved several paces to the rear and, catching Company Sergeant Major Hogben's eye, beckoned to him. He said quietly, 'What do you make of it, Sarn't-Major? You reckon they've called it a day?'

'No way, sir. What's their alternative? A wide sweep to the south. Lose all momentum and then bang into the New Zealand Div? Not on in my book, sir. I'd be willing to bet they're planning some new move. Hope I'm wrong of course and they leave us in peace till the order to pull out. But I wouldn't bet on that. No, sir.'

'That's what I was thinking. Thanks. Somehow it's too damned quiet. We've got to keep on our toes but I don't want the men to tire themselves out watching and waiting. Will you pass the word round, Sarn't Major? I want the platoon commanders to run relays. Half the men on duty for half an hour and the other half resting. And then switch round. And so on. Of course, the moment the balloon goes up, all of them must be in position straightaway. Any questions?'

'No, sir.'

'OK, let's go.'

Five minutes, ten minutes dragged by. Roland stood up and was about to walk back to the signals detachment and send a sitrep to Brigade HQ when Billows, his batman, who had borrowed his field glasses, shouted, 'They're back again, sir!'

There was the raking noise of a hundred whip cracks as concerted fire from the Spandau light machine-guns ripped along the tops of the wadi sides, splashing up puffs of dust and ricocheting whenever they hit a solid object. Four or five men who had poked their heads too high were killed outright. One had a lucky escape when a round skidded off the side of his steel helmet, denting the metal and leaving him with a sore ear and a head that felt a hive of bees had erupted inside it.

Roland had gone to ground about twenty yards away from the wadi's opening. He waited until there was a brief lull in the enemy firing, and then wriggled up the slope, cautiously raising his helmeted head until his eyes were clear of the edge. He saw that under cover of the machine-gun fire, what looked like a platoon of enemy infantry in extended line was zigzagging forward. A third of them were firing sub-machine-guns from the hip as they ran.

When he had carried out his reconnaissance the previous night, he had noticed two large boulders south-west of the wadi opening about fifty yards away. He had written them off in his mind as unlikely enemy cover. Far too close for comfort, in his view. But now it seemed the enemy was intent on using the position as an observation post, and was prepared to lose good men to accomplish it. The Kents had rallied after the initial surprise and were returning fire with effect. Roland saw three or four of the advancing Germans pitch face down under the accurate fusillade.

An observation post for what? The answer came to him with a sickening jolt. Mortar fire, of course. The men in the observation post would have a radio transmitter set with them, and from that close-in distance, they could check each ranging shot from a heavy mortar, telling the main party to adjust their range until each shell was landing fair and square into and along the wadi. And exploding mortar shells would not damage the track the way bombs from the Stuka would do.

But they would certainly damage B Company and its allied troops. Anything clear of the surface – trucks, stores,

124

the RHA guns – would be smashed to ruins. With an expert observer, and Roland would expect that from 90 Light, a mortar shell could be guided almost right into the slit trenches.

Already there came a shriek and a thud, and then a column of dust rose lazily about seventy yards short of the wadi. The first sighting shot from a heavy mortar. A few seconds later, there was another, this time about twenty yards short. By this reckoning, the third should be spot on.

The observation post had to be taken out. The two or three men manning it would have at least one light machine-gun, probably two. To come up out of the safety of the wadi's steep banks and to charge across fifty yards of open terrain would mean probably death and at the very least severe wounds. But it had to be done. What was the old Army motto? 'When in doubt, do something.' Better at least to go down fighting than lying down and waiting to be smashed by heavy mortar fire.

Such thoughts flashed through Roland's mind. He was about to grab the nearest bren-gunner and a couple of his mates and lead them over the top when a shout from Private Quested made him jerk around. 'You fucking idiot,' was the cry. And then, only ten yards away, Roland saw Scrivener grabbing a couple of Mills grenades, one in each hand, and scramble over the wadi's edge.

He broke into a trot, zigzagging as he went, holding one of the grenades in his right hand, fingers pressing down the lever. Ten, fifteen yards he managed before the first burst of gunfire caught him high up on the left shoulder, whirling him round and knocking him down with the force of impact. He staggered up to his knees and then with a superhuman effort, lurched almost upright and stumbled another five paces forward. A second burst caught him, this time in the midriff. He crashed down again. Roland reckoned he must be done for. But, God, what bravery. He felt a pricking in his eyes and it was not the sun's glare or the perennial sand.

Just then, Scrivener stirred once more. Slowly, agonisingly slowly, he managed to raise himself on his left elbow. His right arm came over in a perfect spin bowler's arc, releasing the grenade at the apex. It rose high in the air, glinting in the sun as it lazily arced over the boulders protecting the observation post and dropped between them. It was on a five-second fuse – and four had already been used up. The forward troops had been gripped in silence by the sight of Scrivener's single-handed assault, so the blast of the grenade sounded even louder than usual. A column of bloody dust rose in the still air and bits of equipment soared into the sky.

There was a keening noise coming from deep within Quested. Before anyone could stop him, he fixed bayonets and went charging into no man's land right up to the observation post. Roland could just see him, half-hidden by the boulders, lunging with his bayonet at the dead and the dying German observers. There was some desultory fire from the 90 Light forward sections but Quested walked back, mission accomplished. He had finished off the bastards who had dared to kill his friend. Slinging his rifle on his right shoulder, on reaching Scrivener's body, he stooped down and picked him up, cradling him in both arms as he walked the last twenty yards or so back to the wadi.

Once there, he laid the body gently on the sandy slope. He looked Roland straight in the eye. As his company commander, Roland was too experienced an officer to tear him off a strip for disobeying orders and putting his own life at unnecessary risk. This was a high moment – and Roland was not going to spoil it.

'Is he dead, sir, do you reckon?'

Roland looked at the open, unfocussed eyes, the bloody shirt and the inert limbs. 'Afraid so. That last burst must have got him and he bowled the grenade out of sheer reflex. What fantastic courage! Of course, I'll put him in for a medal – the VC even.'

'But that won't bring him back. He did say he'd be killed today.'

Until then Roland had forgotten his arguments with Scrivener early in the morning and the man's quiet certainty. The reminder jolted him. Was it just one of those things or had he gone and committed suicide to make his prophecy come true? Roland's mind jerked back to Haifa and the old crone in a darkened room. Was her prediction about to come true as well? He felt a chill under the blazing sun.

He said to Quested, 'Why don't you and Groombridge carry his body back to the far end of the wadi? Captain Glenister can arrange to have it looked after properly. We can see it goes back on the first transport to leave later this afternoon. Get the padre to give Scrivener a proper burial. Right, don't hang around. We'll need you both back here as soon as possible.'

For the next ten minutes or so, there was more desultory mortar fire from the Afrika Korps but with their observation post taken out, the mortar shells landed short and wide of the target. Then there was a lull that lasted close on quarter of an hour.

Roland sent a runner to the rear of the wadi to ask Captain Glenister to come forward for a quick meeting. He silently cursed himself for failing to think of telling Quested to pass the message on. That would have saved an extra man having to leave the active front. In the normal way, he thought, I'd have automatically done that. His mind flashed back over two years, back to the In and Out where Scrivener had been propping up the bar in his borrowed squadron leader's uniform. Maybe it was his fault. Maybe by listening to his uncle's advice to report him, the private soldier's subsequent imprisonment had set the inevitable in motion. He shook his head. Get a grip, he thought. There's still a big job to do.

Several minutes passed. Quested and Groombridge returned from their task, but still no sign of Dan. Roland felt himself growing impatient, although common sense told him there was no particular urgency. Finally, Dan did turn up, moving at a semi-trot.

'Sorry about the hold-up,' he said. 'Forgive me. I had to sort out Scrivener's remains. That team of medics wasn't a great help. I hear young Scriv was a bit of a hero.'

'You can say that again. He took out that German OP,' pointing, 'single-handed. I saw it myself – I'm thinking of putting him in for a posthumous VC.'

'Great. Underneath all that bullshit, he was quite a man, I always reckoned.'

'Now then, Dan. There's a bit of a lull on right now but any minute Jerry could come storming back again. What's the time now? OK, close on sixteen-hundred hours. Another four to five hours at least before they might call it a day. There could be a couple of flat-out assaults before then. And we've got to hold the wadi, come what may.

'The troops up this end have borne the brunt to date. Dan, I want you to work out a rota. Bring a section or two at a time forward to replace half the men up front and, when they've settled in, switch the other halves. Got it?'

'All clear.'

'Good. How're things back there?'

'Frankly, verging on boring. The chaps stay in their positions all right, watching the front, full magazines and one up the spout – but nothing much has happened. We thought at first there'd be some fun with those jokers who tried to tackle the salt flats but they gave up too soon. No, switching to the sharp end will buck 'em up.'

'I'm going to get on the blower and talk to HQ. Dan, I'd like you to stand by and listen to the conversation. I'm going to recommend Scrivener for a posthumous VC and Quested for a Military Medal. I want a witness present, just in case I don't survive the rearguard.'

'Bollocks! With due respect, of course.'

'Nice of you, Dan, but you never know. Better to be safe than sorry.'

They walked back to the signals truck, which was largely obscured and protected by a fold in the side of the wadi. The radio transmitter set was close to the tailboard but a crude aerial with a wire attached was sticking up level with the wadi's crest. The signals sergeant was brooding over the crackling set like a mother with a fractious child.

Roland pulled off his steel helmet and put on a spare set of earphones plugged into the radio. 'Get me through to Battalion HQ, would you, sergeant. I want to speak to someone in authority. The adjutant or preferably the CO if he's available. On you go.'

After some to-ing and fro-ing and cryptic verbiage, the sergeant finally said, 'The adjutant's on the air, sir. Your turn to transmit.'

'What the hell's the code name for the Battalion?'

The sergeant flipped a switch and then said softly, as though the whole Afrika Korps were kneeling alongside the wadi's edges, ears straining for the Eighth Army's secrets, 'Medway, sir.'

'Medway, indeed. Christ, what a give-away! Well, here goes.' As the sergeant flipped the switch down, Roland said, 'Medway, calling Medway. This is Scorpion leader speaking. Do you hear me? Over.'

Dan could not distinguish any sense from the crackle of words escaping from the spare headset but it seemed Medway could hear Scorpion leader loud and clear. Roland then gave a concise report, detailing the events to date, the number killed and wounded and the general standard of morale, which he described as high. Dan gave him the thumbs-up sign in agreement. Then Roland described how Private Scrivener had single-handedly taken out the German observation post and how his friend, Private Quested, had advanced under fire to finish off the job with his bayonet and to bring Scrivener's body back from no man's land.

'Look, Ian,' he said. Dan knew he must be speaking to the adjutant, the only Ian in or around Battalion HQ. 'All I can say is this,' Roland went on, 'we've seen a good bit of action this past couple of years. And this is the biggest act of courage I've ever seen. Sarn't Major Hogben agrees. And he can add Dunkirk as experience. I want to recommend Scrivener for a posthumous VC, and Quested, who came through without a scratch, should be in for a Military Medal at the least. Got all that? Over.'

There was more crackling from the headset and then Roland responded rather abruptly, 'Ian, it's not wise to discuss the enemy's plans on air. The man on the spot knows best when to move and when to stay put. I must get back to my post. Remember what I said about Scrivener and Quested. Over and out.' He snatched off the headset and left it dangling. He turned to the sergeant and asked, 'How long did that transmission last?'

'A good five minutes, sir.'

'Too long. You know this better than me but haven't Rommel's signal corps got some machine that closes in on frequencies?'

'Yeah, I think you're right, sir.'

'Well the last thing we want is them listening in on our plans. So, sergeant, I want you to close down transmission. Stay right off the air until I, or Captain Glenister here if I'm not available, give the word to open up again.' Seeing the perplexed look on the man's face, he added, 'That's an order.'

'Right, sir.' He flicked several switches on the radio transmitter set. The crackling noise stopped.

As they walked back towards the sharp end, Dan said, 'That was a bit heavy, wasn't it? What secret plans are there? We either stay put or we withdraw. And after a couple of goes, Jerry must know pretty well what's holding him up. I don't get it.'

'All right. I had to say something to convince that signals sergeant. Look, Dan, as soon as the transmitter's working, battalion HQ will be tempted to get on the blower and tell us what to do every five minutes. And how the hell can they read the situation when they're ten miles and more away? We were selected for this job. Let's for Christ's sake run it the way it should be run. You with me?'

Dan was worried stiff but he did not want to risk adding to the pressure on his commanding officer by arguing the toss. There was no way Battalion or Brigade Headquarters was going to interfere with Roland's conduct of the rearguard. How the hell could they? Out of sight many miles away, they wouldn't have any idea of the situation. But back at Brigade and Division and Corps HQs, they would know what the Scorpion team didn't know – the overall picture. Once the main body of the Eighth Army had closed up and begun to establish solid defences, the order would be passed down the line until it reached the Kents' order group for Operation Scorpion to withdraw. Surely that was the very reason why the radio transmitter set had to be kept open. At some point in the next three to four hours, Scorpion might well be commanded to engage in an orderly retreat.

And now Major Lapledge had closed down the wireless circuit prematurely. Delving into the haze of his memory brought on by too much whisky the night before, Dan vaguely recalled Roland's talk of a soothsayer in – where was it? – Haifa. And her mention of 'The Song of Roland'. The present set-up had reminded this Roland of the poem's plot. And that Roland had refused to blow his magical trumpet to summon back Charlemagne's army so the whole rearguard had been wiped out by the treacherous foe. Bloody hell! Was Roland Lapledge, consciously or unconsciously, trying to repeat history? He would have to confront him and try to persuade him to re-open the radio transmitter link. But now was probably not the right moment. In any case, battalion HQ was highly unlikely to be recalling Scorpion just yet. Or are you being a fucking coward? he asked himself, and looking for excuses to avoid a showdown? Perhaps the tension on Roland would ease off as time passed. Balls, was the silent answer to that one. Rommel would come again, any minute. He had to. There were barely three hours of daylight left.

As if on cue, the bren-guns further forward opened up with Joss' troop of mobile field guns close behind. Choosing a sighting spot where the wadi bellied out, Dan could see a flotilla of panzers, thirty or forty perhaps, charging from the dead ground across the plain. They were firing seventy-five-millimetre rounds over open sights. The shells blasted across the top of the wadi, driving shock waves ahead of them with ear-bursting velocity. One landed on an external bank near the top edge of the wadi, a few yards from where Dan was lying prone. It left a neat furrow in the now compacted sand. The blast jerked Dan's whole body an inch off the sandy slope before it dropped back again; his near ear felt like it been hit by Tommy Farr.

Then, through buzzing ears, he heard the high-pitched scream of a seventy-five-millimetre shell ricocheting off the muzzle of a Royal Horse Artillery gun. Joss Abbeyfield was crouched to the rear. A razor-sharp splinter struck his extended left arm and sliced it clean off. The impact was such that the arm landed three or four feet away. Blood pumped out of the severed artery in a crimson stream.

Joss looked at Dan, who was scrambling towards him. He clutched at the stump with his right hand. The blood splashed his desert boots. 'Making the dust a bit richer,' he said with a grin. Then he collapsed. His sergeant caught him and laid him gently on a groundsheet that had been covering spare ammo. Dan, crouching low as enemy shells were still blasting through the air at head height, ran to the medical dressing station, and explained the situation as he panted to get his breath back. Two orderlies grabbed a folding stretcher and a large medical bag and followed him back to where Joss Abbeyfield lay. The late afternoon was still hot but the knowledgeable sergeant had wrapped a blanket around the wounded man's body, leaving only the severed arm exposed. He knew how severe shock can so often freeze the system. The sergeant had also made a tourniquet out of a lanyard to stem the arterial flow.

Joss was still conscious but his face had gone almost green as the shock took hold and the blood drained away in spurts. One orderly gave him a shot of morphia while the other tied off the artery and one or two bigger veins that were oozing blood. The senior one gave Dan a questioning look.

Dan said, 'Take him back to the dressing station, will you? The order is for no transport to leave just yet. So look after him as best you can. He and his fellows have done us proud.'

The orderly nodded. Dan waved farewell but Joss was unconscious with the shock and the morphia on top. Dan wondered, as he moved quickly back to the mobile guns' position, what the one-armed youngster would be like if he survived the war. Would that carefree, almost careless, attitude also survive? With all the pitying glances and older folk rushing up to help him out of a chair? And, for fuck's sake, how would he even tie a tie with only one hand and a four-inch stump? Did they have artificial arms back in Blighty?

The gunner sergeant had taken command of the troop. Calmly, coldly even, he was indicating targets for the guns still in action. But, as Dan watched from his previous vantage point, it appeared a losing action. Three or four enemy tanks had been stopped, dense smoke from one on fire billowed across the battlefield, but the others, more than thirty, were still grinding their way forward, guns flashing. A dozen of them had made a wide detour to the south where they hoped to be in dead ground and were creeping up the steepish gradient. A chance enemy shell smashed into another of the RHA armoured carriers, fortunately causing no casualties but putting the gun itself out of action, and leaving the defences with only one heavy gun to fight off a host. Bren-gun and rifle fire would just bounce off the thickly-armoured sides of the approaching panzers.

There was a brief lull in the enemy fire. Dan could see something glinting on the ground. Moving closer, he realised it was a gold signet ring on the little finger of Joss' severed arm, catching the light as the sun moved lower in the south-west. The dusty sand where the arm had fallen was already staining the exposed raw flesh. The main bone was exuding some greyish matter. The ring might be a family heirloom, handed down from father to son. It must go back with Joss. On an impulse, Dan stooped and picked up the arm. Not knowing how heavy it would be, he almost dropped it straight back down on the bloodstained dust. Half the size but it must have been at least the weight of a Lee Enfield rifle, what with the bone and muscles and solid flesh.

He called to the gunner sergeant, 'Know anything about this ring of Mr Abbeyfield's?'

'Only that he always wore it, sir. He used to joke that if all else failed, he could always flog it. It's got the family crest on it.'

'Sounds pretty valuable.' Dan was easing the ring off the finger as he spoke. The knuckle seemed swollen; it took some heaving and twisting to get it clear. 'Look, my next job's to inspect the medical tent. Would you like me to take it back and have it put on the little finger of Mr Abbeyfield's good hand?'

'Would you, sir? That would be great.'

Further forward, Private Quested was lying behind Scrivener's bren-gun, which he had taken over when his friend died. The CSM had passed the word round: 'Don't waste ammo. Every shot must be aimed at a real target.' There were very few reserves. Two hundred clips of .303 for the rifles, five rounds to a clip, and about thirty magazines of .303, averaging about twenty-five rounds to a magazine for the brens. Share that lot out between the hundred or so defenders and it worked out at about ten rounds per man. If they had to hold out for another three hours and then perhaps have to fight their way out, it was a scanty reserve.

Private Groombridge was alongside Quested. 'Fuck this for a lark,' he said.

'Groomy, change the record. You've been fucking that lark all the afternoon. Look out for infantry following up behind the tanks.'

'Did you mean it when you said we might get together. After the war, I mean.'

'You should know me by now. I keep my promises.'

'That's bloody great. You doing the growing, me doing the selling. It's the old one-two. They won't know what hit 'em.'

'You won't know what hit you if you don't watch your front.'

'You reckon the skipper knows what the fuck he's doing?'

'The Major's a tough bastard but he knows what's what. The family's well known in our part of Kent. They've produced a lot of good fighting men over the... Bloody hell, just look at those crafty buggers!' Quested peered along the sights of the bren, aiming at a group of 90 Light on foot who were emerging from behind a tank a furlong away. He fired one short burst, then another. Groombridge saw them scatter. Three fell to the ground and never got up again.

'Fuckin' hell,' he said. 'You're good. Up there with old Scriv.' He was moving a spare magazine nearer the gun and did not see how Quested's right hand clenched on the pistol grip, while his forefinger pointed rigidly along the stock. The loss of a friend was still too raw.

Ten yards away, Roland was kneeling up on the slope, swivelling his field glasses to take in the whole area of attack. The tanks were still creeping forward and although his front line of men were picking off the occasional foot soldier who strayed from behind the advancing panzers, as Quested had just done, he knew they could not hold out much longer. The enemy fire was getting even more intense, shells blasting across the top of the wadi or sending up spouts of sand as they smashed into the outside rims. He glanced at his wrist-watch. Seventeen forty-eight. Nearly three hours to go before dusk and then darkness blanketed the fighting zone. He reckoned B Company could last out another twenty minutes, half an hour if Jerry moved cautiously. And he would have failed to carry out orders.

Behind his bitter thoughts, he could just make out the faint drone of a distant aircraft. Christ, he thought, that bloody Stuka's back, this time to shit on us from not too great a height. And it's brought a friend along to join in the fun! That's all I need!

The aircraft flew closer, swooping down as they neared the wadi from the east. But there was none of the howling din that signified a Stuka dive-bombing. And no bombs, either. As the leading aircraft levelled out thirty or forty feet above ground, its cannons opened up, raking the line of panzers. The cannon shells must be armour-piercing, Roland thought, as he saw several enemy tanks lurch sideways under the impact and at least three burst into flames, sending black smoke billowing across the battlefield. As the leading aircraft soared skywards at the end of its run, he saw the hump-backed profile of a Hurricane pinned against the sky for a fleeting second. And then the second Hurricane dived at the tanks that were tackling the steep contours south-west of the wadi. Calculating that they were in dead ground and safe from the defenders' heavy guns, the commander had let his panzers close in too much. They were a sitting target for the marauding tank-busters which attacked them in turn. The damage was even greater than in the first sortie. Spandau machine-guns were turned skywards and a hail of rounds poured up, but the two Hurricanes were up and away, apparently untouched. Indeed, one of them moved out over the sea and, as it flew back eastwards, performed a victory roll. He knew that the manoeuvre was banned in Britain, in case, unbeknown to the pilot, his plane had sustained structural damage during the 'scramble' and the plane crashed out of control. But Roland's heart lifted when he saw the gesture. Bloody hell, he thought, those two achieved more in five minutes than we have in ten hours.

The enemy firing became sporadic and then stopped. Those panzers that were still mobile turned and drove back to safety in the dead ground. They left around over a dozen smouldering and broken hulks in no man's land. A giant transporter appeared in the distance and ambled over to a more superficially damaged tank. Men disembarked to attach strong chains. Quested was taking aim when Roland leant forward and touched his shoulder. 'Forget it,' he said. 'No long-range shooting. We've got to conserve ammo.'

Roland breathed out slowly. Thanks to the Hurricanes – who the hell had sent them? – he was in with a chance.

9

19.05 hours, 27 June 1942

Another hour had quietly passed. Dan was touring his area for the umpteenth time when Private Billows, Roland's batman and runner, came lumbering down the narrow track. 'OC's conference nineteen-fifteen hours, sir. That's ten minutes from now.'

'Thank you, Billows. I do know how the twenty-four hour clock works.'

'Always ready to oblige, sir,' the batman said with a grin.

'And where's it being held?'

'Didn't I say? Up front, sir. In the danger area.'

Dan half raised his boot in a mock gesture and Billows skipped away, still with the same cheeky grin.

As he walked slowly on, Dan made a crucial decision. It was to commit the act no decent soldier should ever do – disobey his commanding officer's orders. He approached the signals truck and beckoned to the sergeant in charge who was squatting by the lowered tailboard. He jumped down and came over. Dan said, his voice steady, not giving away any of the unease he was feeling, 'I want you to switch the R/T set on and then get on to HQ. See if we've missed any reports or orders.'

'But, sir, the Major told me to keep off the air. You heard him.'

'And I'm telling you now to get back on the air.'

The sergeant looked down and twisted the toe of his boot in the sand. At last, he said haltingly, 'You're putting me on the spot, sir. The Major's in overall charge here and his order was very clear. Get off the air and stay off.'

'You're wasting time, sergeant. The situation's changed since Major Lapledge gave that order. I'm now reversing it. And as he told you, if he wasn't available, you take orders from me. So get back on to HQ – now! That's a direct order. Understand?'

The sergeant looked surly, shrugged and walked back to the truck. Dan followed. As the sergeant slowly removed his steel helmet and pulled on a pair of earphones, Dan noticed a spare set plugged into the machine. He too removed his helmet and slipped them on. He was not going to be fooled by excuses or made-up transmissions.

After some crackling and whooping noises and the customary minor adjustments of dials, contact was established. 'This is Operation Scorpion reporting in. I say again, Operation Scorpion. Have you any messages for me? Over.'

'Scorpion, this is Medway Operator. Where the fuck you bin? We've been trying to get through to you this past hour. Standby for two important messages. I say again, standby. Over.'

'Roger, HQ, Roger. Over.'

'Both messages are for OC Scorpion. You must make certain they get to him. Message one as follows: OC Scorpion may withdraw his troops in stages any time from now. They are to proceed eastwards keeping close to the existing track for five miles. An LRDG team will meet them at the RV and lead them to Battalion HQ. Message two states that in any event Operation Scorpion will evacuate its present position not later than twenty-hundred hours and will rejoin us exactly as set out in message one. Any questions? Over.'

The signals sergeant looked questioningly at Dan, who mouthed, 'Ask him to run through it again.' This he did.

After the 'over and out' ritual, Dan exclaimed, 'Well, that's a turn-up for the books. Happy you got through now? Hey, I must dash – OC's conference. Keep that piece of news to yourself, sergeant. The OC's got to clear it first.'

Walking away, he glanced at his wrist-watch. Hell, it was nineteen-fifteen already and he knew what a stickler Roland was for punctuality. He broke into a loping trot but, even so, caught a glare from his OC when he arrived. Naturally, Sergeant-Major Hogben had been on time. He and Roland were huddled on the side of a slope ten or fifteen yards from the nearest soldier.

'Nice of you to turn up.' Heavy sarcasm from his leader.

'Terribly sorry, sir. I got held up at the signals truck.'

'I don't follow. We're off the air. That was my last word of command to the signals.'

'Well, you see, sir...' began Dan, but Roland cut in before he could explain.

'We haven't got all day, so forget it. I accept your apology. Now let's get on with it. Here's the plan. You, Dan, are in charge of all the ancillary troops, signals, the sappers, the dressing station and so forth. You are to withdraw them, along with what's left of Number Three Platoon as cover at twenty-hundred hours. In instalments, of course. The sun will be setting by then, so you should make your getaway without much problem. Keep going, using the track as the guideline, for two hours. If you've reached HQ by then, great. If not, bivouac for the night and press on first thing in the morning.

'Make sure your men have full water bottles and emergency rations, won't you? In fact, the supply truck can join your other vehicles. In which case, Sarn't Major, I want you to make sure that the other two platoons staying put fill their water bottles and draw emergency rations as well.

'Sergeant-Major Hogben will act as linkman. Dan, you will want to go ahead with your leading troops so he will stay here and supervise the withdrawal. When you are all away, he will rejoin the rest of us. You with me?'

'But what happens to the rest of you?'

'This. I feel in my guts that Jerry's going to have one last throw before he packs in for the night. Knowing how precise they are, it could well be on the dot of twenty-hundred hours. That's a thought. OK, change of plan. Start your withdrawal at nineteen-forty-five. We may need the CSM doing his stuff up front on the hour.'

'And what's your intention?'

'To hold the wadi until at least twenty-one-hundred hours. It should be pretty dark by then. We stay put for one more hour, just in case, and pull out at twenty-two-hundred. That's the long and the short of it.'

'Well, sir, I have some news for you. Orders came through from HQ just now to withdraw, lock, stock and barrel, at twenty-hundred hours,' Dan said.

'What the...' and then Roland caught the Sergeant-Major's narrowed gaze switching from one officer's face to the other's. 'All right, Sarn't Major, any questions?'

Slowly, 'No, sir.'

'Fine. You'd better get back and keep an eye on the men. Thank you.'

The moment Hogben was out of earshot, Roland, furious, said, 'What the hell's going on, Dan? I told signals to go off the air and stay off.'

'And I told him to get back on again. Just as well. HQ – code name Medway, if you please – were wondering what the hell had happened. They'd been trying to contact us for hours. Operation Scorpion is to close down at twenty-hundred hours tonight. The whole shooting match, not just the ancillaries. So, in another thirty-five minutes, we'll have done our stuff.'

'Dan, you're a real bastard!' said Roland, his voice ominously quiet. 'That was a direct order I gave that sergeant. I'm the senior officer here. As long as I'm around, that order stands. And you pulled rank on the poor mutt. I thought you were a friend. Christ, you could be on a serious charge. Disobeying a senior officer on active service.'

'Going to bring in the firing squad, sir? You talk about disobeying orders. HQ is senior to you. Are you going to disobey that clear order?'

'I never received that order. Not in person. I've only got your word for it. How do I know you aren't making the whole thing up?'

Dan ignored the obvious dig and stuck to the facts. 'So why not check with the signals sergeant? He'll confirm it. All troops out by twenty-hundred. Those are the CO's orders.'

'And how the hell can the CO read the situation right here in the wadi? He and the Brigadier and all the brass must be a dozen or more miles away right now. All they know is the last R/T message I sent way back. The situation could be changed completely. They won't have a clue.'

'But, Roland, that's the whole point. Division will know the overall plan and will have passed the word down. They may need us back there urgently.'

'And they may not. Look, the retreat – that's what it was, not a withdrawal – was an utter shambles. You know it, you were there. Don't talk to me about grand plans. Eighth Army's on the run and it's my job to stay here and give them a clear start.'

'Is there no way I can convince you, Roland?'

'We're not in the mess now, Captain Glenister, we're in action. So I'd drop the Christian names, if I were you. You read me?'

'Loud and clear, sir. May I make one last point?'

'If you're brief. We've got to get cracking.'

'You're planning to keep back thirty or so men. Aren't you risking their lives unnecessarily?'

'So the news hasn't reached you yet. There's a war on, Glenister.' The heavy sarcasm was back. 'Men who enlist in the infantry learn to expect all the shit that's flying around the sharp end. It's their job. Join the bleeding hearts' brigade if you like but don't expect any easy options round here.'

Dan felt his self-control slipping. 'So you are going to flout orders from above. Just to follow that old woman in Haifa and her prophecy. You're crazy.'

149

'Right, that's enough! That's rank insubordination. I could have you put under arrest. Right now!'

'But you won't, sir. Because if we both survive and I'm court-martialled, the true facts would emerge. And Major Lapledge would be dismissed the service.'

Roland paused, and then, 'Get the hell out of here before I change my mind.' His face softened under the shade of the steel helmet, 'And good luck, Dan.'

'Good luck to you, Roland.'

As Dan walked back towards the service area, he saw CSM Hogben waiting, close to the point where the wadi widened out. Hogben took one look at his face and said, 'Problems, sir?'

'Haven't we all?' Then he took a deep breath. He had to make one last desperate attempt, and he knew that if anyone had influence with Roland, it was the Sergeant Major. 'This is between us. OK?' He sketched out the facts, the radio-transmitter message from HQ and Major Lapledge's refusal to accept the orders to withdraw on the grounds that he had not personally received the message.

'Which is all balls, as you well know, Sergeant-Major. He's got a bee in his bonnet about holding the fort until twenty-one-hundred hours. Crazy! And even if Jerry were to attack a little after twenty-hundred and found the wadi empty, he's not exactly going to dash along the track and attack the main body at dawn tomorrow. No chance. You've seen the damage the RHA did, and then with those two tank-busters, there are still panzers dotted around the landscape. They'll take a while before they're ready for a major attack.'

'So what do you want me to do, sir?'

'Persuade the Major to accept the order to withdraw by twenty-hundred hours.'

CSM Hogben pursed his lips in a soundless whistle.

'That's asking a lot, sir. You know as well as I do what the Major's like when he makes a decision.'

'But it could be sheer bloody suicide for the ones left behind!'

'Don't I know, sir. I'm one of them.'

'Well, if you get the chance, Sarn't Major, do try to put a word in. I must get cracking. And you, too. Here's hoping they hold off till tomorrow morning.'

'I wouldn't bet the old family home on it, sir.'

Dan went to tell his batman to pack up his gear and carry it to the east end of the wadi. He saw Lieutenant Penfold, whose platoon was currently 'resting' from front-line duties, and called him over. He told him to get his men ready to move out in the next ten minutes. One section was to provide cover in front of the slow-moving train of vehicles and men on foot, with a couple of scouts well out in front. Another section would bring up the rear, with Penfold himself in charge. He, Dan, as overall leader of the convoy would either be in the leading truck or on foot with the advance section. The medical truck, the signals truck

151

and the supplies truck would proceed in single file at twenty-yard intervals.

'Think of a cricket pitch, Penfold,' he said.

'I played tennis at school,' came the prim response.

Jesus Christ, Dan thought, no wonder we're almost two years into the war without a victory on land to speak of. Aloud he said, 'Then think of the length of a tennis court.' He told Penfold to have his men standing by but keeping watch till the last possible moment in case of enemy attack.

Corporal Lakri Wood was placed in charge of the supplies truck. Dan told him to be prepared to move out but first to shift half the reserve ammunition boxes and two gallons of water forward under the control of CSM Hogben. 'In fact, put four men onto it. Saves time. If you need more men, bag 'em from Lieutenant Penfold's platoon. Tell him I ordered it.'

'Right-oh, sir. C'mon you bunch of camel-fuckers. Get moving!'

Dan moved the short distance to the Royal Horse Artillery stand. Only one of the three armoured fighting vehicles was still ready for action, the other two having been smashed in the earlier concerted fire of the seventy-five-millimetres. Three men had been wounded, one badly, and had joined Joss Abbeyfield at the dressing station. Sergeant Campbell was checking over the surviving AFV, testing the elevation wheel and the swivelling action of the twenty-five pounder gun. He stopped as Dan told him to get ready for immediate withdrawal.

'We all moving out, sir?' the sergeant asked, nodding his head towards the defenders up front.

'No, sergeant. The Major and one platoon are staying back in case of another attack tonight.'

'With respect, sir, either your Major's crazy or he's looking for a medal. Maybe both.'

'Thank you, sergeant. I shall ignore that last remark.'

'I've seen too many fucking stupid actions in this bloody war. Still, from all accounts it's not as bad as the last one. Great consolation, that.'

Dan's last port of call was the advance dressing station. As he arrived two orderlies were lowering the tent and folding the canvas into sections. The three seriously wounded men on stretchers had been gently moved into the shade. Since the sun was now very low in the sky, the shadows were falling in inky pools on the lower slopes of the wadi's south-west bank. Already, there was a faint chill in the air. Please God, Dan thought for the umpteenth time, Jerry calls it a day and waits till tomorrow for the next attack.

'How's Mr Abbeyfield?' he asked an orderly.

'Who, sir? Oh, the one without the left arm. Not too good, sir. We've kept him sedated but he sounds a bit delirious. Keeps going on about birds and flying.'

'May I see him? It won't take a moment.'

'Of course, sir. He's over there in the shade.'

Dan followed the orderly's pointing finger and found Joss' stretcher which was the furthest one from him. Joss was lying on his back, eyes closed. His face was very flushed and, although he was in the coolest spot in the whole wadi, there were beads of sweat on his forehead. He had one blanket wrapped round him which hid the remaining stump of his arm. Dan suddenly remembered the signet ring. He took it out of his breast pocket, pulled the blanket back until it exposed the good arm, and started pushing the ring onto Joss' little finger. It needed quite an effort to get it over the knuckle.

Joss' eyelids rolled back. At first Dan could have sworn he winked, but then remembered it could have been a tic brought on by the shock of the amputation. As he looked down at him, Joss started to sing in a clear falsetto:

'Cottleston, Cottleston, Cottleston Pie,

A fly can't bird, but a bird can fly.'

And then, in a puzzled tone, he said, 'But can it fly on one wing? That is the question.' His eyes rolled back, the lids closed down and he was back in the morphia-induced sleep.

Walking away, Dan thought bitterly, there's no justice. To lose an arm in your early twenties, to be pestered by sympathisers talking in hushed tones, to be an object of pity. All the worse when it happened to such a dynamic young man with wit and panache. He pulled himself up swiftly. Stop getting maudlin, he told himself. Get the bloody convoy sorted out.

Time was running out. It was already almost nineteen-forty-five hours and they had to be clear of the wadi and on their way not later than twenty-hundred. He summoned Lieutenant Penfold as commanding officer of the platoon, and various fairly senior NCOs, Lakri Wood amongst them, along with representatives from Signals, the RHA and the sappers.

The orders were short and straightforward. Mr Penfold would supply one section to act as scouts in front. As many as possible of his other men were to fill the vehicles. The latter would travel in low gear, so as not to overrun the scouts, and with a minimum of fifty yards between trucks.

'There must be no, repeat no, bunching up. I doubt the Luftwaffe will be active at this time of night but if a single Stuka did happen to be swanning around, he could finish off the lot of you if you're too close together. So keep your distance! And no lights at all. The moon will be really bright in the next hour or so. Finally, Mr Penfold, tell your scouts that the LRDG will be contacting us five miles or so along the track. They will lead us to our billet for the night. Any questions? Right, let's get cracking.'

Dan took his place in the passenger seat of the leading fifteen-hundred weight truck. As with all vehicles destined for the desert campaign, the windscreen had been removed to avoid reflecting sunlight and giving its position away to

the enemy. So a pleasantly cooling breeze played around
Dan's face as the truck moved off.

They hadn't gone far before a problem he had not
foreseen struck home. For a moment he cursed himself for
not having anticipated it. Even grinding along in bottom
gear, the vehicles could not go much slower than five or six
miles an hour without getting stuck in the shifting sands
that had blown across the track. But the footsloggers,
walking in single file on either side of the track, could not
go any faster than three to four miles an hour. So every few
minutes Dan had to stand up in the front of the leading
truck, raise his hand and give the Eighth Army signal to
halt. The trucks would then pull up in sequence and halt
long enough for the troops on foot to catch up. With the
moon now rising and shedding its pale, eerie light, and
knowing that they were all alone in what seemed a vast
empty desert, and that an Afrika Korps ambush could be
waiting round the next corner, they all felt weak and
vulnerable.

When the convoy had travelled perhaps one and a half
miles away from the wadi, Dan thought he heard the
distant crackle of gunfire. The driver alongside was Private
Bell, always known as 'Ding-dong'. He was a small, ferrety
man who smelled faintly of motor oil.

'What did you make of that, Ding-dong?'

'Made of what, sir?'

'Wasn't that gunfire, back at the wadi? At least, I thought I heard what sounded like automatic fire. If so, Jerry must have put in that last attack after all.'

'All I can 'ear, sir, is this sweet little engine turning over. Getting us away from all those nasty bangs.'

'And what about the fellows stuck back there? Spare a thought for them – it could be pretty hairy.'

' 'Alf their luck, sir. This man's army, you're a proper mug if you volunteer for anything. Just stand there, that's what I say, and if someone senior gives you an order, you do it. But no order, no action. That's my philo-whatsit.'

'Point taken, Ding-dong. Now you concentrate on keeping us on the right track.' Smiling, he added, 'And that's an order. So don't fuck about. OK?'

'You got it, sir.'

Another hour passed as the convoy crawled eastwards. There had been one moment of confusion when the track wound in and out around minor cliffs in the escarpment. Because Dan was up front, he could not see what was happening halfway back, but the message soon reached him that a big thirty-hundredweight truck had steered off the track into a patch of soft sand. It had to be dug out, using sand trays and shovels. The high areas around were casting inky pools of darkness but the diggers dared not light up the scene with a torch. The whole convoy fell into turmoil and had to wait nearly ten minutes before a crowd of tugging and shoving men, sweating hard in the cool night air, had managed to ease the bogged-down truck back on to hard ground.

Dan knew better than to start effing and blinding at the guilty driver. Even with vehicles passing along it, the track was quickly obscured with patches of blown sand, and it was the devil's own job to determine where the verges lay, particularly in the pale moonlight and with the track's twists and turns. It was just one of those things. And it would have been a lot worse if the heavy truck had toppled onto its side. Without lifting gear in the convoy, it would then have been a write-off.

Some fifteen minutes later, one of the scouts came trotting back. Panting, he said, 'There's a problem back there, sir. A fork in the track and a bunch of Arabs crouching down. Do we attack 'em, sir?'

Dan replied, 'Hewitson, isn't it? No, Hewitson, they aren't Arabs. That's the Long Range Desert Group, you clown. They often wear keffiyehs in action. You attack them and I'll soon be writing a "Your son died bravely" letter back home to your mum. Got it?'

'Yessir.'

Dan stepped down from the truck and walked back with the scout. He had to admit to himself that the three crouching men in keffiyehs, their jeep hidden in a dip in the ground, did look remarkably like the Bedouin Arabs who so often frequented the far edges of the western desert. As he came closer, they stood up. He could see they were wearing full equipment under their robes. By the time he was almost level with them and could see the jeep, he noticed a machine-gun mounted at the rear. So this was the famous Long Range Desert Group.

'Hi,' he said, 'I'm Captain Glenister, in charge of this convoy. Is any one of you an officer?'

A deeply tanned, rather swarthy, young man with bright eyes, stepped forward. Dan could pick out the white-purple-white ribbon of the Military Cross on his bush shirt. 'I'm Captain Williams,' he said. 'Ex-Queens. You're the Kents, aren't you?'

'That's right, part of B Company, 1st Kents. Plus a few signals, sappers and a medical team. With a few seriously wounded men on the medical truck.'

'Fine. Now this is the plan – if you agree, of course.'

'Shoot.'

'You see the track splits right here. The northern section continues to follow the coast, while this other one forks away south-eastwards. That's the one we'll be using. The bivouac is about ten to twelve miles away.' The moon was much brighter now and he could see Dan's face slump. 'Not to worry. We'll work in a kind of relay. The trucks drive as quickly as is reasonable to the bivouac, discharge their loads and come back to pick up the footsloggers who will have been marching slowly along the track. They drive 'em to the bivouac and then come back to pick up any

surplus. Your lads will have walked far enough tonight. In
the end, they'll all get a lift. Approved?'

'Absolutely. A first-class plan. Will you and your men be
staying with us overnight?'

'Afraid not. Once we know you're installed and have
signalled the news back to base, we've got to reconnoitre
the Wadi Minquar and see what happened to Rommel's
last go.'

Dan's mind had been much occupied with looking after
his convoy. For an hour or so he had stopped worrying
about Roland and Hogben and the other good men
carrying out the final stand. Please God, he thought, let
them come through. Captain Williams had been foraging
in the back of his jeep. He came back, clutching a bottle of
whisky by the neck.

'Here,' he said, 'get a load of this. Gets a bit nippy in the
high desert these nights.'

'Sure you can spare it?'

'No problem! First thing they taught us when we joined
this outfit. Always keep spares!' His smile caught the
moonlight.

He went on, 'Just for the record, you are the last lot out
of the Wadi Minquar, aren't you? You must have had to
fight your way out. Way back, we thought we heard
automatic and mortar fire ever so faintly.'

Dan's stomach felt hollow – and not from hunger. There
was no point in lying; a lie would be discovered the

160

moment they did their recce. 'No,' he said. 'The company commander, Major Lapledge, and one platoon stayed put. In case there was one last attack before dark.'

'But that's crazy. Orders came through from division.' He indicated the radio-transmitter set on the jeep and added, 'We've stayed netted to Div and your battalion HQ throughout the manoeuvre. Around nineteen-thirty hours the order came through – and it was acknowledged by Operation Scorpion – to withdraw not later than twenty-hundred. I don't get it.'

'You're not suggesting I abandoned my post and brought the men out prematurely, are you? The OC told me to move them out – and that's what I did.'

'Sure, sure. I'm not suggesting anything. It's just a bit weird, that's all. Well, let's not hang around. Would you start moving the men in?'

The LRDG had spotted an abandoned defensive position with trenches still usable and a couple of Italian sangars on adjacent high ground. Several of the men were glancing towards them when their captain warned them off. 'I'd avoid the sangars if I were you. You know what the Eye-ties can be like. Don't build latrines, just crap where you are. There's a stench up there worse than a whore's armpit.'

Soon the different sections began arriving and Dan mechanically dispersed them, making sure that Joss, now in a deep sleep, was gently lowered from the medical truck;

but his mind kept going back to Roland and his too few troops. Had they made a fighting withdrawal? Had they – only God knew how – driven the enemy back one last time? Or had Rommel squashed them like a real-life scorpion underfoot? And that bloody signals set. He wished he'd smashed it.

10

20.22 hours, 27 June 1942

The last act, when it came, was brutal, bloody and brief. They could not have known it at the time but there was to be a twenty-five minute interval when the rising moon grew steadily brighter and stars began to prick the dark foreboding sky with brilliant dots. The men had had one last brew-up and were swilling down their corned beef and dry biscuit rations with gulps of hot, sweet tea. The outside temperature was dropping fast and their sweat-soaked shirts felt cold and clammy in the breezes coming in off the nearby sea. One by one, they unstrapped their packs, pulled out their sweaters, carefully removed their equipment, pulled the sweaters over their heads and then refitted their fighting gear.

There was almost one complete platoon plus three men from company headquarters, including Billows the batman. Adding in himself and the CSM, Roland made it a total of thirty-five. He looked at them, almost with affection, as they lolled against the various sides of the wadi, waiting patiently. He remembered a fragment of Shakespeare – 'We few, we precious few'. How very apt! Looking at them now, he recalled the dreadful shock he and his fellow officers had felt two years earlier when, many miles away from the action, they had heard that Paris had fallen and that the German forces were marching through La Place de la Concorde. And then, perhaps a week or so later, he had received a letter from his mother. 'We are in the final now!' she had written. 'Now it's us against them. I never did trust those French.' You wonderful idiot, he had thought. It's just like the club tennis competition to you. The Germans may batter away at England but they'll never conquer that level of stupidity.

Roland decided to address the men, something he had never done before during his career as an officer. He asked CSM Hogben to arrange a couple of lookouts and then to assemble the rest of them in a group, sitting down. The moment the CSM reported, 'Everyone present and correct, sir', Roland, still standing, began, 'All right, at ease. This is a talk, not a speech. We've got one last job to do – and you're the men I've chosen to do it.

'By denying Jerry the track that runs through this wadi, we are giving the rest of the Eighth Army a breathing space, a chance to choose strong defensive positions without having to duck the whole time or shoot back. You fellows have done a great job so far. And there's just one

164

more job to do. That is: hold this position for,' he glanced at the luminous dial of his wrist-watch, 'another hour and five minutes. Now it could be they've given up for the night and we just sit here twiddling our thumbs. But if they do put up a show, it's up to us to see them off. So keep on the alert the whole time.

'The rest of B Company under Captain Glenister has moved back to our stop over for the rest of the night with the various bits and pieces. Another hour, and we'll be on our way to join them. It all depends on 1st Kents right now. So let's show 'em what 1st Kents can do.' He paused, and then, 'All right, men, that's it. At ease. Only an hour to go.'

He moved away and beckoned to CSM Hogben, who went over and said quietly, 'That should put some lead in their pencils, sir.'

'Glad you think so, Sarn't Major. A thought's struck me. Now the rearward half has moved out, we've got no one guarding the wadi back where it broadens out. You can't put it past the crafty Hun to circle round and attack us from the rear. A real bit of buggery, you might say. So would you take one of the three sections and spread them in good defensive positions. I want you to stay back there, take command of that half, the eastern half, of the wadi. If they do attack us, you must act as you see fit, depending on the state of play. You with me?'

'Right-oh, sir. One problem though, we're pretty short of ammo. I make it there are two spare magazines for each bren and about ten rounds apiece for the riflemen. Plus a couple of dozen Mills grenades.'

'Not a lot. You're dead right. Ummm. OK, they'll just have to conserve their ammunition. No firing by rifle at tanks. Sheer waste of a round. And the bren-gunners must copy that brave young fellow, Scrivener. Straight aim and short bursts. You got me? Good. Then spread the word right now, would you? Fine. That'll be all for now. Oh, and good luck, Piggy.' He held out his hand and gripped the CSM's battle-hard palm and fingers. Hogben smiled and walked away to carry out his instructions.

A strange feeling was slipping into Roland. He felt excited and elated, the way he had felt as a very young subaltern, straight out of Sandhurst and travelling by P&O liner to join the 1st Battalion in India. A shipboard flirtation with a major's wife going out to be with her husband in the Royal Engineers had led to his first ever experience of physical love. He remembered that very same feeling from the time when, after sharing a bottle of wine at dinner and passionate kisses on the upper deck afterwards, he had waited till the coast was clear and had then slipped along the corridor to tap discreetly on the door of her cabin.

And yet this time he also had an overriding sense of calm, of fulfilment. It was as though everything in his life had inevitably led up to this moment. He did not regret ordering Dan to move out with the majority of B

Company. They had fought a good fight and now would live to fight another day. He did feel a pang at the thought of the thirty-five men he had held back to carry on the fight if the Afrika Korps did have one more go that night. Their lives would be at risk. But that was par for the course, as he had said to Dan, if you joined the infantry in a major war. It was usually first into action and last out.

He glanced at some of them as they sat, backs against the slope of the wadi's sides. There was old Shakesy Roberts, already a raucous corporal when he, Roland, had joined 1st Kents in a cantonment outside Delhi way back in 1935. Good man, Shakesy – once you got past all the bullshit, the stamping of highly polished boots, the bellowing shouts that nearly split your eardrums, the quivering salute and the exaggerated deference that hid a caustic wit.

Where was Daffy Norman, the fitness freak, who was never far from Shakesy? Oh yes, he remembered now. Daffy was in the section that had moved to the rear of the wadi with CSM Hogben. When Daffy had first joined the battalion in Egypt eighteen months ago, he could do thirty or more consecutive press-ups, wearing full fighting gear including a steel helmet. He could force march six miles in an hour, again kitted out for action. He was the fittest man in the whole battalion. And then every complaint liable to hit an Eighth Army man had descended on poor Daffy: amoebic dysentery, desert sores, heat exhaustion, bacillary dysentery. Not one of the officers or senior NCOs could understand why such a paragon should succumb so easily. He certainly wasn't playing up. He had been proud of his extreme fitness and was crestfallen at the loss of it.

On a visit to divisional HQ, Roland had found himself sitting next to a full colonel in the Royal Army Medical Corps. His hair was grey, his face lined, he spoke slowly between puffs on an old briar pipe. Roland mentioned the case of Daffy Norman and asked his advice.

'Back in Harley Street, m'boy, this would cost you a packet. All right, I'll settle for another scotch and soda.' A pause while the orderly refilled his glass. 'Your good health, sir. It's quite simple, really. Now, tell me, young man, do you weigh yourself regularly?'

'Fairly regularly, sir.'

'Good. What weight were you when you first landed in Egypt?'

Roland had thought hard for a moment. 'Twelve stone nine, sir. Twelve ten, perhaps.'

'And what weight are you now?'

'Just over twelve. Say, twelve two at the most.'

'There you are. Have you suffered any of these ailments? Dysentery, heat exhaustion?'

'No, sir. Touch wood.'

The Colonel had blown out a long spiral of grey smoke. 'That's it. Case proven. Any man dropped into this kind of sweltering climate needs a reserve. You can't help sweating your guts out when the temperature hits ninety, a hundred, a hundred and ten, perhaps. By the time you've acclimatised, you have sweated off that reserve and are now completely fit. As you have done. But your Mr Norman had worked off his reserve before he ever got here. All those press-ups. The man's a blithering idiot. When the heat and the unsanitary conditions hit him, he had nothing to fall back on. Hence he was a sitting target. Those fitness courses back home are a sheer waste of time. You're an infantryman, I see. 1st Kents – good regiment. Fighting will get you fit, if the climate hasn't done it already. Good luck, m'boy. Here, don't hang around. Much longer and you'll force me to buy you a drink in return. Have the free advice instead.'

This all seemed so long ago now. Two full years. Mussolini's men, stationed in Tripoli, had invaded Libya and briefly captured the townships of Sollum and Bardia. The Kents had been shipped out to reinforce the Eighth Army and to learn what desert fighting was all about. Mussolini's troops were not, apart from the Folgore Division, ardent warriors and the initial blooding was easy. But then Hitler had despatched General Rommel and the Afrika Korps who proved themselves to be a hardened professional fighting force. With better guns, including the deadly eighty-eight-millimetre adapted from its original anti-aircraft use, and more modern tanks, the bold German commander had cut deep into the Eighth Army. For eighteen months it had been a war fought on the back foot, gallant tank crews dying in vain because the armour plating needed at least another inch of thickness and the guns were not powerful enough.

The mobile infantry had played its part. Tanks might gain a position but they still needed men on the ground to go in and clean up, to capture or kill the few remaining defenders. Roland knew he had been lucky. So far! He had taken part in all too many fighting patrols at night, and daytime attacks in 'thin-skinned' vehicles. Whilst others had been wounded or killed, he had not suffered a scratch. A shell splinter had once torn through the left arm roll-up of his sleeve, leaving a series of jagged tears when the sleeve was unrolled but that was the closest he had ever come to being wounded. Half your luck, as the army saying went. He knew that if he had been standing just six inches further to his left, that would have been it. He would never have known what killed him.

And then it started. A piercing whistle, followed by the thump of an explosion, and then a plume of smoke and sand sprouting from the desert floor twenty-five yards short of the damaged tank slewed round in the opening to the wadi. Another, one, two, three, four more and then a rain of mortar shells creeping ever closer to the defences.

'Down! Down!' Roland yelled, as he dived into his slit trench. Billows, his batman, was already cowering in one corner, knees drawn up to his chest.

'Turned out nice again, sir,' he said.

170

Roland couldn't think of a witty reply. In any case, the shrieking of the mortar shells and their thunderous blast would have drowned out any such attempt. He felt his shoulder blades instinctively shrink together as the giant drum strokes crashed ever closer. The earth shook and on a level with his eyes, he saw a trickle of sand descend like a dry waterfall down the steep side of the trench. One shell must have landed right into a nearby trench. Half on his back and gazing up at the moonlit sky, Roland saw half a leg with the boot, stocking and puttee still intact, go sailing up in the air, followed by a spray of flesh, bits of bone and many splashes of blood.

After five more minutes the barrage stopped as abruptly as it had started. Roland scrambled out of the slit trench, dragging a reluctant Billows with him. He knew all too well that the attack usually came in as soon as the barrage had softened up the defence. And sure enough, he could see figures perhaps a hundred yards away moving at a slow trot towards their objective – the wadi. 'Right,' he shouted, 'back to your positions. On the double! Move it.'

Quested was already in position, bren-gun cocked and aimed. Groombridge was alongside him, clutching a spare magazine. He looked pale in the moonlight and was shivering uncontrollably. Roland, making a mental note to keep an eye on him, said, 'Well done, Quested. You too, Groombridge. Start shooting. Choose your own targets, OK? And remember – conserve ammo. No long bursts.'

171

He moved around the platoon, urging them on, encouraging them, watching the results of their shooting. Considering the moonlight played tricks with vision, often making objects appear much further away than they actually were, he thought the marksmen were doing pretty well, Quested and his bren-gun in particular. About twenty of the Afrika Korps on foot, 90th Light, no doubt, had been dropped. But still the rest came nearer. They were now almost on a level with the bunch of rocks that had briefly served them as an observation post until Scrivener had taken them out. But that meant the enemy was only fifty yards away now, only a few seconds' dash when the blood was up.

Quested's countryman's eyes were tuned in to the elements. 'Sir,' he shouted, 'I've seen a lot of them going into dead ground that way,' pointing south. 'You think they might be circling around to attack us in the rear?'

'The pansies,' added Groombridge.

'· Roland ignored him. 'Good point, Quested. Here, Billows, you're a spare file. Nip back and give my compliments to CSM Hogben. Ask him to keep a special watch out for a possible attack. Oh, and when you get there, you can stay back and help Mr Hogben out. Got it? Nothing much for you to do at this end of things.'

But Private Billows never completed his mission. He had only gone about ten yards down the track when a German sergeant ran forward under cover of the smashed tank, vaulted up by its turret, saw the figure disappearing in the distance and fired a burst from his machine pistol. Billows stopped short as though he had run into a brick wall and then crashed down on to the track, dead. Roland was already gripping his Smith & Wesson revolver but before he could take aim, Quested swung up on one knee and fired a three-round burst that took the German high in the chest and knocked him back off the tank.

And then it all happened. In the half light, German soldiers began to swarm up the outer slopes of the wadi. Silhouetted against the sky, they made great targets. To the defenders, it was like potting ducks in a shooting gallery. But still they kept coming. As one wave fell, another wave swept over their grounded bodies. Foot by foot, they were advancing. Roland's men had to leave the imagined safety of their slit trenches as the attackers crashed in above them.

Roland shouted, 'Fix bayonets! Come on, lads, let's show 'em some cold steel!' A fleeting thought – how fucking theatrical can you get? – crossed his mind. But the men responded. He had emptied his revolver; it would take too long to spin the cylinder and feed in one round at a time. He took a pace back and stumbled over a body that had rolled down off the slope. The man's bayonet was still in its scabbard. Without conscious thought, Roland stooped and slid the bayonet free. He waved it in the air, and with a concerted howl, his men charged in a bunch.

Quested had emptied the last magazine. He snatched up the bren-gun by its muzzle, not heeding that it was almost red hot and beginning to burn his palms, and swung it like a two-fisted club.

He sent an Afrika Korps sergeant reeling, blood spurting from a broken nose, and smashed another enemy's upper right arm. He was grunting and keening in his rage. And then, as he drew back to deliver another mighty blow, an officer from 90th Light, crouching a few paces away, levelled his Luger pistol and fired once, twice, at the base of Quested's neck. His body thumped down on the soft sand. His big frame twitched twice and then was still in death.

Groombridge had been ducking and diving just behind Quested, using him as a shield. When he saw his friend go down, he fell alongside, eyes shut, feigning death. Once Jerry captured the wadi, and he reckoned that it would be in only a matter of minutes, those still alive would be taken prisoner. He'd had enough of this fucking war. No girls, no fun, no bright lights. At least in a POW camp, he'd get proper meals three times a day and a bed to sleep in. And now his friend was dead. That put an end to their dream, the fruit farm they would run together after the war, old Bill doing the growing and him the selling to snazzy places like the Savoy and Fortnum's. He felt sick and tears pricked his eyes under the closed lids.

Roland was stabbing and hacking away with the bayonet in his hand. The platoon – what was left of them – charged and charged again, yelling, almost screaming with fear-braced drive. At one moment, it seemed they had thrown back the enemy, who regrouped behind the shelter of the broken-down tank. But they drove back again, relentlessly and now it was the turn of the Kents platoon to give ground. One of the Afrika Korps, a bull of a man, grabbed up a British rifle with bayonet fixed, dropped by a dead Kent. He lunged forward, grunting. Roland, who had won a fencing competition years before at Sandhurst, swivelled, and the blade of the attacking bayonet speared past his left hip. Then, gripping his own bayonet, he slammed it into the German, who was so near he could feel the man's hot breath on his face. The bayonet sank in, his enemy groaned and fell back, dropping the Lee Enfield rifle and clutching at his stomach. Roland jammed his left foot on the man's waist to give himself some leverage and heaved back the bayonet. It exited the wound with an audible squelch. The man doubled his knees up against his chest and lay there groaning.

Roland, ignoring him, swung a quick look to either side. He felt separated from the platoon, the remnants of which had herded themselves into a tight little band, their backs against one of the wadi's steeper slopes. About to fight his way over to join them, Roland suddenly felt a thump and a searing pain in his guts. He glanced down and saw a rifle, supported on its butt, protruding from his lower chest. Somehow, the wounded German had made one convulsive

175

dying movement, half charging with, half launching, the rifle and bayonet at his enemy. Roland flung his own bayonet at the man on the ground and, using both hands, tried to pull the muzzle of the rifle with its fixed bayonet out of his body. But his eyes had gone vague and he heard a roaring in his ears. His legs could no longer hold his weight. They buckled and he slipped down, down, until his back hit the sandy slope. He lay there, vacant eyes fixed on the night sky, his life slowly ebbing away. Perhaps luckily, he was beyond conscious thought.

With only ten men and a largish area to control, CSM Hogben knew he had problems. Jerry was unlikely to risk the black ooze of the salt flats to the north of the wadi – but with Rommel's troops, you just never knew. He would have to place one lookout on that side and at least one other on the more likely approach on the south side. That left eight men plus himself to hold the fort. It might work out in a boys' magazine but Hogben knew several hundred attackers would not be held at bay for more than minutes.

In the desert air, he and his section could hear the crackle and rattle of machine-guns and the occasional grenade explosion when the attack came in on the west side of the wadi. After a short while, the high-pitched bursts of Spandau fire took the leading role as, one by one, the brens stopped firing. They could just hear the Major yelling something about bayonets and then a short silence fell. So the bayonets were at work, putting the fear of God into the enemy. Who was he kidding? Twenty men – or what was left of them – with twelve inches of cold steel apiece were not about to send an army running.

Just then, one of the southern lookouts shouted, 'Mr Hogben! Sir! They're coming. Masses of 'em.'

The CSM bounded up the slope alongside the man. Shit, they were coming without a doubt. There must have been at least two full companies a hundred yards away, flitting at the half double in and out of the inky shadows on the southern side. His men might take out two or three times their own number but he knew the battle was lost before it began. He could sign their death warrant, his own as well, no doubt, but for what? The Major should have evacuated the wadi by twenty-hundred hours but, for some perverse reason of his own, he had hung on too long. And there were some good men gone as a result. Hogben refused to add to their number.

'Right,' he shouted, 'listen hard. Drop your weapons and raise your arms in the air. I say again – drop your weapons and raise your arms in the air. We're going to surrender. Stand well clear of each other, so as Jerry can see at a glance we've chucked it in.'

He stood there, head up, chin in, with his arms above his head as the first wave of attackers swept over the crest. His men followed suit.

Epilogue

18.25 hours, 19 August 1942

The Eighth Army had established itself along the Alamein line by mid-July and fought off prolonged and bitter attacks by the Afrika Korps. The fiercest fighting had been directed at Ruweisat Ridge, a knuckle of rock that stuck out about halfway between the sea and the Qattara Depression. The 4th Indian Division and the New Zealand Division bore much of the brunt, each suffering many casualties. But Rommel's supply lines were overstretched, his tanks needed overhauling, his men were tired. So he drew back a short distance, laid minefields as a buffer and built up his reserves for more attacks.

Meanwhile, GHQ Middle East Forces back in Cairo was stirring. General Wavell, the General Officer Commanding, felt it necessary to dismiss General Auchinleck as commander of the Eighth Army. General Sir Alan Brooke, Chief of the Imperial General Staff in Whitehall, arrived in Cairo, followed by the Prime Minister himself, Winston

179

Churchill. They gave Wavell, an intelligent and humane man, the chop and General Alexander was summoned from the United Kingdom to take his place. General Gott, an attacker by nature, and always known as 'Strafer' Gott, was chosen to lead the Eighth Army in his place, but was killed before he could take up the appointment. The aircraft carrying him to Cairo was shot down. So Lieutenant-General Bernard Montgomery was selected to fill the dead man's shoes.

In a major British war, those in command at the outset suffer the worst luck. The vital ingredients for winning battles – modern tanks, accurate heavy guns, sufficient well-trained troops – are almost always lacking. General Gort, commander of Home Forces, suffered dismissal after Dunkirk; Wavell in the Middle East not only had to supervise fighting on two separate fronts at the same time, but was given wholly inadequate weapons and too few men for the task. He was kicked upstairs to become Viceroy of India but the Army had been his life.

And now, when improvements were made, it was to be Montgomery who was to benefit. Eighth Army was to be enlarged – 44th (Home Counties) Division had arrived in Egypt a few weeks earlier and was already manning part of the Alamein line, with the 51st Highland Division close behind. The latest Sherman tanks with their thicker armour plate and bigger guns were rolling off the merchant ships in Port Said. There was a buzz in the air.

Because of B Company's heavy losses during Operation Scorpion, 1st Kents had spent less than a week in the Alamein defences and had then been drawn further back in reserve, a few miles west of Alexandria. The other two battalions in the brigade had also suffered quite heavy casualties and were stationed close by. It so happened that both the CO and the Brigadier had been ordered to report to GHQ in Cairo, but had travelled there separately. In turn they had checked into Shepherds Hotel, enjoyed the luxury of lying for half an hour in a large bath with the fan circling lazily overhead and then changing into the crackle of clean starched bush jackets. And now they had met at the long bar and were enjoying that first long drink of the early evening.

The CO broke their silent reverie. 'This meeting tomorrow with the Military Secretary. Obviously, something to do with a change of job. You're good at keeping your ear to the ground, Hoppy. Any idea what it's all about?'

'Yes, as it happens. But for God's sake, don't tell a soul. And look surprised when the MS breaks the news tomorrow. You've got my job.'

The CO let his breath out in a whistle. 'You're pulling my leg!'

'Cross my heart, Mike.'

'Well, that's great! Dinner tonight's on me. But, hey, what's happening to you, Hoppy? Are you free to say?'

'Why not? But with the same proviso – lips sealed until after the meeting tomorrow. I was given a choice. I could go back to the UK to command a brigade there – keeping the same rank as now, of course. Or I could be promoted to major-general and command a district in northern Palestine. It was a real bugger. I was in India when war was declared and my wife and kids were shipped home during the phoney war. When Mussolini declared war in June '40 my battalion – I was then a company commander – was moved to Egypt and I've been stuck here ever since. Haven't seen the family for almost three years. And the way the war's going, it could be another three before I do.'

'So why not opt for the Blighty job?'

'Simple. When the war does finally come to an end, the Regular Army will revert to being a smallish force. Every officer will drop down at least one wartime rank. Lieutenant-colonels will revert to majors, majors will become captains, and so on. I know it sounds crazy thinking of salaries and pension rights in a major war like this one but that's what it's all about in the long run.'

'You'll get no promotion this side of the ocean, so cheer up, my lads, fuck 'em all,' the CO chanted softly. After long abstinence, the drinks were beginning to get to him. The two lapsed into silence.

When the Brigadier finally did speak, the CO was surprised by the bitterness in his voice. 'And now Monty's turned up,' he said. 'Trust him!'

'Monty's not one of your pin-ups, then?'

'As the saying goes, "not bloody likely". One way or another, we're all ambitious, I suppose, but there are limits. Monty was stationed in Palestine when war was declared. The way I've heard it he wasn't going to hang around in a backwater when the real action would be in Europe, so he had himself invalided home. Taken on board the ship on a stretcher, if you please! But the sea breezes must have worked a miraculous recovery, for by the time the ship docked in Southampton, he was fighting fit and rarin' to go.'

The CO hiccuped and then said, 'Mind you, way back when he first became a brigadier, word was he had a private line direct to the Almighty.'

'He certainly behaved that way. I'll tell you a personal reason why I'd like to wring the little bastard's neck. I've got an older brother – he inherited the brains in the family! He was forty, an up-and-coming barrister, back in September 1939. He was a patriot who volunteered for the Army right off, just when the big fees were beginning to roll in. Could have walked into a cushy job with the Judge Advocate General's department, advising on the knottier points of law at courts martial. But no, it was the infantry for him. He scrambled through the officers' training course and was posted to a young soldiers' battalion in Kent. The 70th Battalion The Buffs, in fact. Monty was GOC 13th

Corps and it so happened that 70th Buffs came under his direct command.

'After an inspection, he took the CO aside and said in that grating voice of his, "Yours is a bad battalion. There are no bad soldiers, only bad officers. You have some thirty officers, of whom I judge at least twelve are bad. I shall call here next Saturday, shortly before eleven-hundred hours. You will give me a list of your twelve worst officers and have them standing by. Sharp at eleven-hundred hours, I shall start interviewing them individually. Each man will have exactly five minutes, no more, no less, to make his case. At the end of the hour, I shall give you a list of those who shall leave the battalion forthwith."

'And so it was. My poor brother – for once his eloquence deserted him. I believe ten out of the twelve were given the chop, him included. They were apparently men like himself who loved their country and wanted to fight for it, even though they were older and probably less fit than the average officer. Oh yes, Monty may have been right – 70th Buffs with young officer replacements was a lot brisker after the blood bath – but the way he did it gets my goat. Judge, jury and executioner all rolled up in one.'

Despite the effects the alcohol was having on him, the CO could see that this was a raw nerve. He decided to change the subject. 'Come on, Mike. If we sit here much longer, I shall either cry into my empty glass or slide gracefully under the table. Let's find our table and eat.'

Dinner over, the Brigadier leaned back in his chair, drew on his cigar until the end glowed, and twirled his wineglass. 'Living rough for months is a great way to make you appreciate the finer things in life when you do get 'em. What do they call GHQ staff officers? Groppi's Light Horse – after that wonderful cake shop and café along the street. Here's hoping Haifa has something equally good.'

Now the Brigadier had relaxed again, the CO took his chance, 'Look, Hoppy, we've been tiptoeing around it for too long. Operation Scorpion, I mean. I lost my best company commander, two of my junior officers were taken prisoner, one badly wounded, and another thirty killed or put in the bag. A whole company ripped to pieces. And what happens? We put in for some medals – a posthumous VC for Private Scrivener who stormed a defensive position single-handed, a posthumous DSO for the company commander, Major Lapledge, and a few other lesser decorations. Silence. It felt like farting in church. Finally, Scrivener is downgraded to a Military Medal and Roland Lapledge – or his family – gets an MC. Off the record, you tell me why.'

'I could suggest Scrivener's spell in the glasshouse for masquerading as a fighter pilot had something to do with it.'

'Oh, come off it! I may have had a spot too much to drink but my bullshit detector's still working. If that's the case, why was the Major's medal downgraded? Being late on parade?'

The Brigadier looked at him sharply. 'Mike, you're picking at a delicate situation. It really isn't something I should discuss. But seeing you'll be in my job in a few days' time and will have access to the files, I might as well save you the trouble of looking it up.'

'Well?'

'The officer commanding 15 Panzer and 90 Light withdrew them to their previous position, along with thirty or so prisoners. Our dead were left where they fell until daylight hours next day. The LRDG had been observing closely, and after the enemy evacuated the wadi, they quietly flitted through. This next bit is top secret, please note, Mike. They found the Major dead, lying on his back with a British bayonet, still attached to the rifle, sticking out of his chest. OK, OK, please let me finish. There must have been hand-to-hand fighting and yes, of course, it could have been that an Afrika Korps man grabbed the rifle and bayonet and stabbed the Major to death.'

'Or what you're hinting. It could have been one of his own men. In a rage because he hadn't been withdrawn in good time.'

'Well, you said it, Mike. That's one problem. There's another.'

'Christ Almighty!'

'Ease off, Mike. I'm just the bearer of bad tidings. You remember my original orders, and I've no doubt you passed them on accurately to Lapledge and co. If Operation Scorpion was still going strong at twenty-hundred hours on 27 June, the company commander was to pull his men out at once. But it could well be that the order to evacuate would come somewhat earlier.

'So what happens? First of all, Scorpion mysteriously goes off the air. Now only the commanding officer could have given that order. Stop shaking your head, Mike. It stands to reason. The signals sergeant wouldn't take orders from a senior NCO or a platoon commander, or even the second-in-command, Captain Glenister. Anyway, in the court of inquiry, the signals man stated it was the Major who issued the order.

'Glenister was the next crucial witness. He did his best to back the Major but when it came to the pinch he had to admit he had told the signals man to get back on the air. And when the message came through to start clearing out at once, he personally passed it on to the Major, who then sent him and the auxiliary troops packing, along with two platoons of the Kents, leaving the OC and one platoon to hold the fort. That decision signed several death warrants, his own included, and some longish prison sentences.'

'Hell, I never saw it that way,' said the CO.

'I'm sorry about Scrivener. He probably did deserve a VC. But in my book, Major Lapledge is lucky to get any sort of medal.'

'I'd always looked on Roland Lapledge as an ideal company commander. In fact, I thought he'd make a damn good CO for an infantry battalion.'

'Now that's where I part company with you, Mike. You remember way back, before Scorpion, I wanted him to switch to brigade major, if I could shift young Peter, who, incidentally, is still functioning larger than life. He'll be your boy when you take over.'

'Thanks a lot.'

The Brigadier went on, 'Where was I? Oh yes, the real Roland. There was something reckless, almost desperate about him deep down. Perhaps he should have transferred to young Stirling's new mob, the SAS. Maybe that would have suited him better?'

'Perhaps,' said Mike. 'Listen Hoppy, give me your advice on this. There's something that's come back to haunt me since Roland's death. He came to see me once on mobilisation leave to ask permission to marry. He was a regular, still under thirty so, as you know, his CO's permission was required. It seems he had fallen madly in love with a Yank – pretty girl, judging by her photograph. Daughter of an American Embassy official in London. She was twenty, he was four, nearly five years older.

'I went through the usual patter. They were both so young, she'd be on her own for several years probably. She might have to go back to the States if her father's career took him back. We would soon be in action and he'd have to concentrate on the job in hand, not mope around over a new wife back home. You know, Hoppy, the usual CO's stuff. He seemed to take it quite well – but then you never know, knew, with our Roland. But this is what bothers me. If I'd given the go-ahead, then as a married man he might not have been so reckless. He might have pulled out when ordered.'

'Who knows? You know the score, Mike. I don't have to tell you that battle takes men different ways. But listen, don't lose sleep over it – you'll never know now. Here, your glass is empty. Let's have one last port, then it's bed for me. Waiter!'

'You reckon the operation was a cock-up?' asked the CO.

'No way! If it wasn't for Scorpion, we wouldn't be here tonight, enjoying the best grub, washed down by the best wine in Egypt. The defence your boys put up for close on two days was a vital factor. Perhaps *the* vital factor in establishing the Alamein line before Rommel could turn up. And don't just take my word for it. You remember Brigade came under Corps command when we reached Alamein. General Leese is no idiot. When he found out who I was, he made a point of calling me out and congratulating me on the heroic defence – those were his actual words – of your B Company. Without which, he said, the whole Army might have been in a pretty pickle. Most of us thought it was in a bad enough pickle as things were. But the General was right. Those forty-eight hours made all the difference.'

'But I still can't get over having the medals downgraded.'

'*C'est la querre.* If people ask me off the record what I think of the Major's conduct, I say I reckon he was suffering from what the Foreign Legion calls *le cafard.* That little beetle that goes round and round inside your head, ticking away. He'd been up in the blue too long. That was the cause.'

'And his bravery counts for nothing?'

'No, I'm not saying that, Mike. Look, you and I and all those involved know it was a complete shambles. The retreat to Alamein, I mean. Oh yes, the BBC can broadcast, 'withdrawing to previously prepared positions,' and make it sound like a clever game of chess, but you and I know different. It was a demoralised retreat. Back here at GHQ, they want to keep quiet about it. No flag-waving, no big handout of medals. At least, that's my theory.'

'So dead men don't get the honours they deserve just in case it might upset GHQ.'

'Dead men aren't here to wear them with pride.'

'No, but they do have families, and a medal awarded for bravery helps soften the blow of a loved-one's death.

That's my experience and no clever-clever argument is going to change it.'

The Brigadier said softly, 'I wonder if Roland Lapledge's posthumous MC is going to help his mother and father. I'm told it's the end of a family after nearly nine hundred years. His elder brother was in the RAF – "missing, believed killed in action" – and there are no sisters or close relatives it seems. His mother is over fifty so no more kids for her.'

'We've just got to believe Operation Scorpion was worth it'.

'It was, Mike, it really was.'

'I'll drink to that. Here's to Scorpion.' He raised his glass and added with a catch in his throat, 'And good men gone.'

Afterword

The events around which George Greenfield's splendid novel *Rich Dust* is based are the campaigns in the Western Desert in 1942 that marked the turning point of the Second World War. 'Before Alamein we never had a victory,' Churchill once remarked, 'after Alamein we never had a defeat.' That the battle should have been fought at the same time as the Battle of Stalingrad, where Nazi Germany also met with defeat in an utterly different theatre of war, is one of the great coincidences of history. Before El Alamein and Stalingrad, Hitler's armies seemed constantly to be on the offensive, carving out a European and Mediterranean Empire to rival that of Ancient Rome, yet after those two great engagements, the Nazi legions were thrown onto the defensive, as they were forced to start the great retreat that took them back to Berlin itself, and even to 'the beast's lair', as Churchill described the Fuhrerbunker.

The story of the fighting that took the British Army back and forth all along the North-African littoral began on 10 June 1940, when the Italian dictator, Benito Mussolini, suddenly declared war on the British and French Empires. Defending British interests in Egypt, especially the all-important Suez Canal, were only a small British force of 36,000 men. Mussolini hoped that by invading Britain's ally, Egypt, he could gain an easy victory that would win him the admiration of his fellow fascist dictator in Berlin. Therefore on 13 September 1940, the Italian Marshal, Rodolfo Graziani, invaded Egypt with five divisions and took up defensive positions at Mersa Matruh, awaiting the inevitable British response.

On 9 December, General Archibald Wavell unleashed his counter-offensive – Operation Compass – which forced the Italians back five hundred miles and inflicted heavy casualties and utter demoralisation. Rather than Hitler being impressed with the Italian effort in North Africa, he was so concerned about the situation there that the following month he despatched General Erwin Rommel, a panzer-tank commander of genius who had distinguished himself during the fall of France, to command the Afrika Korps, a newly raised armoured group. This decision was entirely to change the complexion of the war in the region.

Rommel's first attack came on 24 March 1941, and showed immediately that he had grasped the principles of desert warfare just as well as he had mastered the tactics of blitzkrieg in France and the Low Countries the previous year. Within a fortnight he had expelled the British from Libya, all except for a garrison defending the port of Tobruk. Wavell responded with Operation Battleaxe, but this was brought to a halt on 17 June at Libya's Halfaya Pass. Wavell was then, perhaps unfairly, replaced by a new British commander, General Sir Claude Auchinleck. Just as Hitler had improvised the new Afrika Corps, so Auchinleck now commanded its newly created British opponent – the Eighth Army.

Auchinleck launched his offensive on 18 November 1941 with Operation Crusader, forcing Rommel, who was running short of essential supplies, to retreat. Yet by January 1942, the Allied advances meant that it was Auchinleck's turn to suffer from over-extended supply lines, and Rommel brilliantly counter-attacked. Tobruk fell to the Germans on 21 June, and the following month the Afrika Korps got to within seventy miles of the vital Egyptian port of Alexandria. The prospect of losing the war in the desert so alarmed Winston Churchill that he flew to Egypt to take personal stock of the situation. He decided that if the Western Desert was to be cleared of Axis troops, and the way left open for an eventual Allied invasion of Italy itself, further changes needed to be made in the Eighth Army's high command. He therefore gave the overall command of all the British and imperial troops in the whole of the Middle East theatre to General Sir Harold

Alexander, with the specific Eighth Army command going to General W H E Gott. When Gott was killed in a plane crash before he was even able to take up his command, the job then went to Lieutenant-General Bernard Montgomery.

The arrival of the prickly, controversial but undoubtedly highly talented Montgomery in North Africa marked a turning point for Allied fortunes there. 'Here we will stand and fight; there will be no further withdrawal,' he told the Eighth Army on assuming command on 13 August 1942. 'I have ordered that all plans and instructions dealing with further withdrawal are to be burned at once. We will stand and fight here. If we can't stay here alive, then let us stay here dead. Meanwhile, we ourselves will start to plan a great offensive; it will be the beginning of a campaign which will hit Rommel and his army for six, right out of Africa.' For all the vainglorious, almost un-British tenor of those statements, Montgomery knew that the myth of Rommel – who was widely respected in the Eighth Army, credited with almost superhuman abilities, and nicknamed 'The Desert Fox' for his cunning – could only be opposed by the myth of another commander of charisma, and so deliberately set about creating the popular legend associated with the name 'Monty'.

Because of their success at penetrating deep into Egypt, the Afrika Corps began experiencing their own severe re-supply difficulties, not least because of the Royal

Navy's superb blockading operations in the southern Mediterranean, operating out of Malta. Even when supplies did get through, convoys from Benghazi and Tripoli in Libya took a week and ten days respectively to reach the front along the sole highway along the coast. Hostile climate conditions and the need to navigate by compass or by native tracks further held up deliveries in other sectors. Furthermore the Allies' Desert Air Force created havoc with the Axis supply operations. Soldiers of both sides were meanwhile subjected to temperatures in the hundreds during the days, but sub-zero during the nights.

Rommel's increasingly desperate requests for German, as opposed to Italian, reinforcements went largely unheeded in the Wehrmacht High Command, so on 30 August he attacked at Alam el Halfa hoping to break Montgomery before he had a chance to settle into his new command. After four days' hard fighting, it became clear that Montgomery had won this first of many battle of the wills, and that Rommel had to withdraw. With the Germans now stuck in a forty-mile bottleneck, with the Mediterranean Sea to the north and the impassable salt marsh, the Qattara Depression, to the south, Montgomery was confident about the next stage of the campaign.

Montgomery was in no hurry to attack, appreciating how his position was inherently stronger than Rommel's and that time was also on his side. He stockpiled arms and ammunition, enforced rigorous training and worked hard to burnish the cult of his own personality that he believed increased morale and confidence in victory. Although Churchill believed that Montgomery should capitalise on the full-moon period in September to follow up the victory at Alam el Halfa, Montgomery refused to bow to his judgment. He bided his time, arguing that October would also see a full moon. Meanwhile he carefully planned for every possible eventuality for the coming attack. Extensive camouflaging and misinformation were employed to try to conceal the fact that the main thrust of the attack along the forty-mile long battle front would, in fact, come from the northern sector rather than the southern.

On 6 October 1942 Montgomery gave his subordinate commanders the following uncompromising instructions for the assault from El Alamein, codenamed Operation Lightfoot: 'It is essential to impress on all officers that determined leadership will be very vital in this battle, as in any battle. There have been far too many unwounded prisoners taken in this war. We must impress on our officers, NCOs and men, that when they are cut off or surrounded, and there appears to be no hope of survival, they must organise themselves into a defensive locality and hold out where they are. By so doing they will add enormously to the enemy's difficulties; they will greatly assist the development of our own operations; and they will save themselves from spending the rest of the war in a prison camp. Nothing is ever hopeless so long as troops have stout hearts, and have weapons and ammunition.'

By the time of the great offensive, and thanks in part to Montgomery's careful shepherding of men and resources, the Eighth Army consisted of no fewer than 195,000 men, 1,351 tanks (including 285 of the new American Sherman tanks), and 1,900 artillery pieces. Against this the Afrika Corps and their Italian allies could only muster 100,000 men, 510 tanks (of which 300 were inferior Italian models) and 1,325 pieces of artillery. Hitler was expecting miracles from Rommel, and he was not providing his general with the wherewithal to perform them. Indeed when the actual attack came, Rommel was on sick-leave in Austria and his temporary replacement, General Georg Stumme, proved even more temporary than expected when he had a heart attack and died while on reconnaissance on the morning of the second day of the Allied offensive. Hitler personally telephoned Rommel to order the 'Desert Fox' back to his post in Egypt as soon as possible.

The Allied artillery barrage which had opened up at 9.40 p.m. on 23 October 1942, constituted the greatest single bombardment seen since the First World War. Yet because of extremely deep German minefields – five miles in some places – and fierce German resistance, by the end of the second day of fighting Montgomery was forced to change his initial plan and make fresh ones. When Rommel returned to the field he launched strong counter-attacks,

199

which were only repulsed on 27 October with a high level of casualties on both sides. On the night of 28/29 October, Montgomery sent the Ninth Australian Division northwards to threaten the vital coastal road, so forcing Rommel to bring up German units from the south to try to hold the road. Churchill, meanwhile, criticised Montgomery for fighting what, from London, looked to him like a 'half-hearted battle'. It was a phrase he was later to regret employing.

On the night of 1/2 November the second phase of the battle began when Rommel realised that the sustained assault of the Eighth Army, now in its tenth day, could no longer be resisted. Allied superiority in numbers and equipment had begun to tell, and by 4 November, a sunny day with a clear blue sky, Rommel was in full retreat. Hitler personally countermanded Rommel's order, saying, from his headquarters deep in Eastern Prussia, 'There can be no other thought but to stand fast and throw every gun and every man into the battle. As to your troops, you can show them no other road than that to victory or death.' Rommel reacted by claiming Hitler's order, 'demanded the impossible. Even the most devoted soldier can be killed by a bomb.' Finally Hitler gave permission to Rommel to withdraw the Axis army to Fuka, sixty miles to the west. Large numbers of Italian infantry were meanwhile taken prisoner.

On 7 November Rommel, with only twenty tanks remaining under his command, reached the Egypt-Libyan border. He learnt the next day that the Allies had made successful seaborne landings in Morocco and Algeria under the command of the American General, Dwight Eisenhower. He was now to be subjected to a war on two fronts. During the twelve-day battle of El Alamein, one of the most decisive military engagements in history, no less than half Rommel's army was killed, wounded or captured, and 450 tanks and over 1,000 guns were captured or destroyed, at the cost of 13,500 Allied casualties. As a direct result Rommel was forced to evacuate North Africa, and the Allies were able to use the region as the springboard for the invasion of Italy. To men like George Greenfield, and his comrades-in-arms, goes the priceless accolade that their heroism in North Africa paved the way for the liberation of Europe, and ultimately for the victory of civilisation over oppression.

Andrew Roberts

HOUSE OF
STRATUS

Internet:	www.houseofstratus.com including synopses and features.
Email:	sales@houseofstratus.com
	info@houseofstratus.com
	(please quote author, title and credit card details.)
Tel:	Order Line
	0800 169 1780 (UK)
	800 724 1100 (USA)
	International
	+44 (0) 1845 527700 (UK)
	+01 845 463 1100 (USA)
Fax:	+44 (0) 1845 527711 (UK)
	+01 845 463 0018 (USA)
	(please quote author, title and credit card details.)
Send to:	House of Stratus Sales Department House of Stratus Inc.
	Thirsk Industrial Park 2 Neptune Road
	York Road, Thirsk Poughkeepsie
	North Yorkshire, YO7 3BX NY 12601
	UK USA